Now I Remember

I Love You

Now I Remember
I Love You

Janet Aird

Alta Press

Cover illustration © 2016 Howard Simpson
Interior book design and layout by
Abba Studios: abbadabba.com

Divider clipart © exactea.com

Printed in the United States of America

First Printing 2017

ISBN 978-0-9981565-0-7

AltaPress
altapress.online

For Mike Malecki

Love always

Prologue

He caresses the back of her hand with his thumb. The wrinkles curve like waves across her thin skin.

She nestles into him. "You've still got it," she says.

He pulls up the sheet and tucks it around her shoulders.

"What are we going to do?" she asks.

"I don't know. But we'll do it together."

Chapter One

Spring, 2001

Nick lies in bed, watching Evie get dressed. Her white hair is thin and wispy now. Her hazel eyes have the same glints of green he fell in love with so many years ago, but crinkles spread out from the corners and down her cheeks. Her breasts sag. Her back curves. And her arms, once strong enough to carry two crying children out of a store like footballs, are mostly bone with loose skin flapping below them. Her clothes hang from her shapeless body.

"I don't know how you can look at me," Evie says. "I've gotten so old."

He holds her from behind and nuzzles her neck. "I get so much pleasure from your body," he says. "How could I not think it's beautiful?"

She leans back against him for a moment, then turns and kisses him on the cheek.

"Go back to bed. I'll make breakfast."

"I'll be down in a minute."

He hasn't left her alone in the kitchen for six months, since she set the stove on fire.

Evie takes eggs, bacon and a carton of orange juice out of the fridge and puts them on the counter. She separates two slices of bread from the loaf and puts them beside the eggs. And then she stands back, looking at them.

"How's it going?" Nick asks.

She looks at him in despair. "I don't know what to do."

"Here," he says. He turns on the burner under the frying pan and hands her the bacon, slice by slice. Once it's cooked, he slips it out of the frying pan onto a paper towel and hands her an egg. He coaches her through the rest of the steps and helps her take the plates to the kitchen table.

"I don't think I'm going to like this part of my life," she says.

But she forges on.

She spends her days taking care of the house. In their bedroom, she empties dresser drawers one by one, spreads the contents on their bed and touches each one. Sometimes she lays a piece of jewelry on one of her sweaters, rolls it up and pats it back into a corner of a drawer. Other times she picks up two or three items and distributes them through the house, gently, deliberately.

Nick finds his watch in with the place mats in the dining room, a toothbrush in his shoe, old letters he wrote to her in a kitchen cupboard, paper clips everywhere.

More and more often, he catches her looking at him, puzzled, as if she can't see him properly. He still thinks of himself as the handsome man she fell in love with all those years ago, and he's always surprised to see in the mirror that, somehow, he has aged. He's still in good shape, except for where his stomach pooches out a little. His curly gray hair has thinned to almost nothing on the top of his head, but his eyebrows have become almost terrifyingly bushy. His skin is still smooth though, and his smile as wide as ever.

The first time she doesn't recognize him they're in the living room, watching the news.

"Who are you?" she asks him.

"I'm Nick," he says. "Your husband."

"You aren't Nick," she says. "You don't look anything like him. You're too old. I want to see Nick."

He feels that dangerous burning behind his eyes, that warning that he's going to shame himself and cry. But he doesn't, not yet. Instead, he calls their son, Kevin.

"Can you please talk to your mother and tell her who I am?" he asks, his voice quavering.

"Hi Mom," Kevin says. "How are you?"

"I'm scared," Evie tells him. "I don't live here. I live in another house, exactly like this one. I don't remember where it is, but Nick is there, waiting for me. This man is nice, but I told him I'd only stay here for four days, and this is the sixth day already. I can't find my suitcase and I don't have a ticket to get home. Can you call Nick and tell him to come and get me?"

"Oh, Mom," Kevin says. "That man is Nick. He's your husband, and he loves you very much."

"He is?"

"I promise you he is."

Kevin can hear Evie talking to Nick. "Kevin says you're my husband. Is that true?"

"Yes," Kevin hears Nick say. "And he's right. I do love you very much."

Evie comes back on the line. "Nick is right here."

"I'm so glad, Mom. It's late. You'd better go to bed."

Kevin calls Kathy, his sister.

"I think it's more than aging," he says. "Do you think she could have what Grandma Landry had?"

"Oh god, I hope not."

"I'll drive up from Santa Barbara on Saturday and see what's going on."

"Thanks, Kevin. I'll try to fly down from San Francisco in a week or two. In the meantime, I'll ask Aiden to drop in on them tomorrow after her last class."

The next day, Aiden, Kathy's nineteen-year old daughter, drives over from the university to see her grandparents. Her eyes are green like her great-grandfather's and almond-shaped like her father's. Bright red streaks wind down her curly brown hair. She slings a backpack over one shoulder and lets Barney, her little spaniel mix, leap out of the car. They both bounce up to the front door.

"Come in, come in." Nick wraps her in a hug. "Grandma's in the kitchen."

"Hello darling." Evie is at the kitchen table, eating scrambled eggs straight from the frying pan. She holds out her hand and Aiden clasps it before she leans down to kiss her.

"It's wonderful of you to take the time to come and see us," Evie says.

Barney drops a tennis ball at Nick's feet. Nick tosses it and Barney races across the living room, skids down the hall floor and scrambles to catch it as it ricochets off a kitchen wall. He drops it in Evie's lap and sits beside her as she fondles his ears.

"It's nice to have a little more life in here," Evie says.

"I'm glad we have a chance to see you," Aiden says. "How are you?"

"We're doing just fine, aren't we, old girl?" Nick turns to Evie.

"Oh yes," Evie says on cue. "We're doing wonderfully."

"Really? That's great. Even last night?"

"Last night? We slept like babies," Nick says.

That evening, Aiden is getting ready for bed when she hears Evie's voice rising. She looks inside their bedroom.

"Grandma, are you okay?"

"Tell this man to get out of my room," Evie says.

Nick's head is bowed. "You take care of her, Aiden," he says. "I'll be downstairs."

Aiden picks up her grandmother's nightie. "Can you put this on by yourself?" she asks.

Evie undoes the buttons of her blouse and starts to pull her arm out of the sleeve, but she can't get her elbow out. The more she twists, the tighter the blouse wraps around her.

"Wait a minute, Grandma," Aiden says. "Here. Let me help."

Moments later, Evie is in her silky pink nightgown. She looks at the bed.

"I don't want to sleep in there with that man."

"He's your husband," Aiden says, "Nick."

"Nick isn't here. He's at home waiting for me. Can you call him and ask him to come and get me?"

Aiden takes a deep breath. "I know this is frightening for you, Grandma," she says, with more understanding than she knew she had, "but this really is your home. All your clothes are here."

She opens the closet door. "See?"

"I want to talk to Nick. Right now."

"He's downstairs, Grandma."

"I want to talk to Kevin then. He'll tell me where Nick is."

Aiden calls him. "Uncle Kevin? Grandma doesn't believe that Grandpa is her husband. Can you please talk to her?"

"Oh, no," Kevin says. "Are you okay?"

"Yeah, but I don't know what to do."

"Honey, your mom and I think she might have Alzheimer's – the same thing Grandma Landry had. Go along with whatever she says."

"Okay, thanks Uncle Kevin. Here's Grandma."

She hands Evie the phone.

"Hello, Kevin?" Evie says. "Can you please give me Nick's phone number? I've been wanting to call him for days but no one here will give it to me."

"He's with you in the house," Aiden hears Kevin say.

"No, he's not," Evie says. "That's Dad. Nick is waiting for me in our other house."

The silence is too long.

"Dad is Nick," Kevin finally says. "They're the same person."

"No, they're not."

Another silence.

"They are, Mom. Nick is your husband and Dad is my father." Kevin pauses. "And Dad is your husband and Nick is my father."

"Dad is my husband?"

"Yes."

Another long silence.

"But what will I do when Nick comes back for me? How can I explain to him that I already have a husband?"

Aiden finds Nick the living room, his face buried in his hands. She crouches down beside his chair. "You know this has nothing to do with you, don't you, Grandpa?"

He desperately wants to believe it. It becomes his mantra, and her disease becomes his life.

1942

Evie was twelve years old when her mother took her to the Girls' Home, where strangers were going to look after her until her

father came back from being a doctor in The War. She didn't know where The War was, but it sounded very far away.

Evie and her mother drove all afternoon to get there from their home in Mariposa, on California's Central Coast. At first, the road was lined with fields of strawberries and bright green winter vegetables – spinach, cabbage, peas. The fields faded into a landscape of withered grasses and shrubs dotted by oak trees, which eventually gave way to the shadows of towering cliffs.

The cliffs opened onto a mesa and a small town. Evie's mother drove through the town and turned down a long gravel driveway to a wide red-brick Victorian mansion. The bottom halves of almost all the windows were boarded up.

Evie clung to her mother's hand as they walked up the gravel driveway.

Her mother was wearing Evie's favorite skirt. Soft blue and white yarns wove in and out, disappearing, reappearing, disappearing again, for as long as Evie looked at it. Her hair was short and curly, and looked soft, soft, soft. Her lipstick was bright red. Evie remembered the way her mother looked for a long time.

Evie was wearing her best dress, the red plaid with the satin bow. She looked up the concrete steps to the huge, wooden double doors and held her mother's hand tighter.

"Come on, Evie," her mother said. "They're waiting for us."

They climbed up together. Her mother pulled open one of the doors and they stepped inside. The hall was big, empty and cold. Not just the air, but something in the air. Evie could feel it.

Straight ahead was a gleaming wooden staircase. On Evie's left, through the glass-paned doors, was the dining hall. Down the hallway on her right an old woman bustled toward them.

"Mrs. Madison?" the woman asked. "I'm Miss Gillard."

"How do you do?" Evie's mother said.

The woman looked down at Evie.

"And who do we have here?" She smiled, but her eyes were hooded and cold. When she talked, spit flew out between her teeth.

Evie's mother nudged her. "What do you say?"

"Evie," Evie whispered.

Miss Gillard bent down close enough to Evie that Evie could see the brown edges of her teeth. "My name is Evelyn Madison, Ma'am," Miss Gillard said. The skin under her chin shook.

"My name is Evelyn Madison, Ma'am," Evie repeated, feeling very small.

"Good girl."

Miss Gillard looked sternly at Evie's mother. "You may go now, Mrs. Madison," she said. "Your staying will only make it harder for Evelyn. Don't worry, we'll take good care of her."

Evie's mother crouched down and wiped the tears rolling down Evie's face. "You be a good girl now," she said. "Daddy and I will come back for you as soon as we can."

A skinny woman in a flowered dress came down the stairs. "This is Evelyn? Evelyn, my name is Miss Evans. Come with me. I'll take you to your room."

Evie turned around. Her mother was gone.

Evie felt a giant fist squeezing her heart as she followed Miss Evans up the staircase. A window at the top was almost as high as she was, but it let in only a murky light. They turned to the left and walked down a dim hallway that had two doors on each side.

Miss Evans stopped at the last door on the right. Inside, ten iron bunk beds lined two walls. Most of the beds were made perfectly smoothly, with gray blankets and dingy white pillows. She walked between the rows to a bed with a narrow striped mattress in the far corner of the room.

"That's yours on top," Miss Evans said. "You may make your bed and put your things away in there." She pointed to the wooden box at the foot of the bottom bunk.

"One of the girls will come and get you when the bell rings for supper. My room is down the hall, so I'll hear if you are misbehaving."

Evie opened her suitcase and transferred her clothes from her old life to her new one. She climbed the ladder slowly, waiting for it to stop shaking before she took each step. At the top, she crawled onto the thin mattress.

She unfolded one of the sheets at the foot of the bed and spread it out. It wasn't easy when she was already on it. She crawled around tugging and pushing the sheets and the itchy gray blankets until they lay mostly flat, then she surveyed the room. Nothing but the two rows of beds, the boxes on the floor, and windows boarded up on the bottom and too grimy to see through on the top.

She lay on her back and touched the cool ceiling with her hands and her feet, pretending she was walking upside down on all fours. Anything to try to keep the icy terror from overtaking her as she waited for one of the girls, whoever she was, to come and get her.

Evie heard a set of footsteps shuffle up the stairs and a gong echo through the bare hallway: ga-dong, ga-dong, ga-dong. And more footsteps, lots of them. They passed her door and clattered down the stairs. She swung her feet around and sat on the bed. One of the girls rushed into her room.

"You the new girl? I'm Debby. Hurry up. We're late."

Evie clambered down. "I'm just staying here until my father gets back from The War," Evie said. "It might even be tomorrow."

"Sure," Debby said. "Whatever you say."

Evie smelled cigarette smoke as she followed her. That was interesting. Evie had smoked before, with her friends in the woods behind her house. Maybe this place wouldn't be so bad, after all.

But it was. Debby and her friends never asked her to smoke with them. They never really looked at her, not even Debby, who slept in the bunk beside hers. But often, Debby's crying woke Evie up at night. Evie never could understand how someone who was so beautiful and popular could be so sad.

Some of the girls actually seemed to like the Home. Evie didn't understand them either. From the time the gong woke them up in the morning, they seemed happy. They talked and laughed after class, before bed, on the weekends. They did their homework in the evening. Their black Oxfords, donated by the local shoe store, were always polished.

The rest of the girls, like Evie, weren't even friends with each other. They spent their days pretending they weren't there. Their bodies moved through the day, but nothing really touched them, at least that's what they thought. They were punished, often, like Debby and her friends were, but instead of laughing it off, these girls just didn't care.

Evie dreaded every day. She always woke up in her cocoon of blankets seconds before she heard a door downstairs creak. Then her heart would fall. The heavy footsteps shuffled up each stair. And at the top of the stairs, the gong of doom. Ga-dong, ga-dong, ga-dong. And another dreary, dreadful day began, of schoolwork and knitting socks for the brave men overseas.

1945

Almost three years after Evie had arrived at the Home, she heard someone running down the hall, banging on the classroom doors and shouting, "The war is over!"

Evie's teacher collapsed in her chair and began to cry. Most of the other girls jumped up and cheered. Evie sat quietly at her desk, too overwhelmed to move.

A few weeks later, she received a letter from her mother. She tore it open:

> My darling Evie,
>   I have wonderful news. Your father is finally coming home!
>   He was badly injured, and his doctors have told him that he needs more rehabilitation and, of course, quiet. We're sure that in a year or two, he will be well enough for you to come home to us.
>   We know that you are old enough to understand. We promise you, we will come and get you as soon as he has recovered.
>   We both love you very much,
>   Mommy

Evie read it again. And again. It always meant the same thing. No, she didn't understand.

Evie listened in despair as most of the other girls talked about going home. She watched in envy as they packed up their few belongings. She sat on the cold stone steps and watched them dance on the front lawn as they waited for their parents, and run to them and jump into their arms. Soon there were only about fifteen girls left.

Evie's heart almost tore apart every time she climbed up the steps back into the gloomy building, up the stairs, down the hall and into the room that just she and Debby shared now. She could have moved to any other bed, but she felt safer in her nest in the corner just below the ceiling.

Sometimes she stared at the photo in her box on the floor. It showed only the heads and shoulders of the couple who would become her parents. He had a long head, with a blond crew cut and green eyes flecked with gold. She had dark curly hair and sparkly brown eyes. His arm sheltered her and her head tilted toward him. Both were smiling the confident smiles of a young couple in love.

When Evie looked at herself in the bathroom mirror, she saw hair that was straight like her father's, but mousy brown and unevenly cut with scissors she'd stolen from the art room at school. Her eyes were hazel, as if they couldn't decide whether to be green or brown, and her skin was pale. Dull, dull, dull. Nothing at all like her gorgeous mother.

One afternoon, Debby asked Evie to steal some cigarettes from the teachers' lounge. Evie waited until the shuffle before dinner, when the teachers had left the lounge and the girls were lining up to go into the dining room.

The girls were forbidden even to look inside the lounge if the door happened to be open. When Evie went in, she discovered why. Although the teachers demanded perfect order from the girls at all times, their lounge was a jumble of sweaters and jackets, brown-lined, lipstick-printed coffee cups and crumb-covered plates. Stacks of newspapers and magazines slid across the floor. Bent cigarette butts studded the ashtrays.

Evie started looking in the jacket pockets, where she used to find her father's cigarettes. She scoured the tables and found a few more packs. She took two or three from each pack, not enough to be noticed. Finally, she checked the ashtrays and took the longest stubbed out butts. She also took some wooden matches from a matchbox.

She closed the door and made her way back to her room, where Debby and her two friends, Louise and Libby, were waiting. Evie dropped the loot onto Debby's bed.

"You're one of us now," Debby said. "You can never tell on us."

Debby lit a cigarette with one of the matches and the others lit theirs from hers. When Debby's cigarette touched Evie's and Evie saw the tiny strands of tobacco at the tip burn bright red, she felt a welling up of happiness she hadn't felt for years.

The teachers who stayed at the Home after the war lost interest in the girls, and Evie began to look forward to each day. Louise and Libby moved into Evie's and Debby's room, and the four friends smoked freely. And although they were never hungry, they began to sneak down to the kitchen in the middle of the night and eat whatever the cooks had baked for the next day.

When Miss Evans turned out her light at night, they'd make their way downstairs by moonlight, through the dining room and into the kitchen. They'd walk into the giant refrigerator and pull out trays of cookies, cakes or loaves of bread, and sit on the floor and gorge themselves until they felt sick.

One night, Louise leaned against a wall in the kitchen, and they heard a buzzer and jerky mechanical sounds from behind it.

"What's this?"

Debby pointed to a switch, and a frame around something that looked like a cupboard door flush with the wall. When they pulled it open, an empty space extended about two feet to the wall in the back. A shelf was attached to ropes on both sides and to some kind of shaft on the back wall.

They looked at each other. Evie flipped the switch. The shelf went down. She flipped it again. It came back up.

She went first, huddling on the shelf with her hands and feet tucked in. Rattling, creaking, grinding. A jerk threw her against the back wall. And the slow descent until the final jolt.

"Oomph."

"Are you okay?" she heard from above.

"Yeah. I'm just going to open...aaaahhh...." She tumbled straight down about three feet onto the dirt floor.

"Evie! Are you okay?"

"Yeah. Come on down. Just be careful when you get out. It's a big step."

Evie heard the dumbwaiter bang its way upward. She got up slowly. At first, it seemed as if there was no light at all, but as her eyes got used to the darkness, she gradually saw parts of the room. It was another kitchen, much bigger and older looking than the one upstairs.

Bang, clunk, and Debby appeared. Debby unrolled herself and Evie helped her down.

"Ready!" And the dumbwaiter banged its way back up again.

"Take a look," Evie said. On the far side of the room was an arched stone fireplace, higher than the girls. On another side was a counter, some ten feet long, with a large, deep sink and a long-handled pump.

Crash, and Libby was in the opening. They helped her out, and last, Louise.

Libby looked around. "My gramma used to work down here when she was a little girl," she said very slowly. "Rich people lived here. She said she used to help the cook make the meals and send them up to the kitchen upstairs. I never understood what she meant."

"Let's see what else is down here," Debby said.

They stepped over broken china and lumps of concrete to the green metal door. As they pushed it open, moonlight slanted through the high windows and lit a long passageway with industrial-sized bulbs hanging by wires on the ceiling. Giant green pipes clanged as they snaked along the ceiling. Specks of dust filtered up from the floor.

The girls walked quietly down the passageway and to the right. There were windows to their left and the clanging was louder now. They passed a set of stairs that led to the outside, and shortly afterward, they found a door where the clanging was loudest.

They opened it slowly and waited for their eyes to adjust to the dark again. The room was full of pipes and wires hooked up to machinery of all shapes. Clanging, banging, whistling filled the room. The noise seemed comforting, somehow. In one corner was a small table, a chair and a mattress with a stained pink satin pillow.

Debby lay down on the mattress. "Let's play jelly belly," she said.

Louise lay with her head on Debby's stomach. Libby lay down and put her head on Louise's stomach. Evie stiffened, terrified and longing for whatever intimacy was coming.

"Come on, Evie!"

She lay down and settled her head on Libby's stomach. Debby moved over and put her head on Evie's. And Evie became part of the soft, warm flesh and the sharp, angled bones on the mattress. As Evie's head moved with each of Libby's breaths, and Debby's moved with hers, the sensation sparked a new feeling in her: desire.

But Louise began to laugh, and Libby's head bounced up and down. Debby laughed, and so did Libby. When Libby's stomach jiggled, Evie laughed, too. Not because she thought it was funny, but because she knew that was what she was supposed to do.

At first she felt uncomfortable, but as her laughter mingled with the others, ebbed and grew strong again in that dark, wild room, Evie began to lose her sense of herself. Instead, she felt herself blending in, disappearing, becoming one with the tangled mass of bodies.

And as she laughed, she noticed a feeling, like a bubble, welling up from her stomach. The feeling burst from her mouth as she laughed and her eyes began to burn. Soon she was sobbing, tears flooding her eyes, washing down her cheeks, into her mouth, her ears, down her neck. And then she realized that all the laughter in the room had turned into the same uncontrollable, cleansing sobs.

Gradually, the sobbing died down. Evie was exhausted and her chest hurt. The ache in her heart was gone, but in its place was a sense that they had done something very wrong.

The girls got up silently and helped each other back up the dumbwaiter. They never mentioned jelly belly again.

1947

When Evie was in twelfth grade, her class was called to the library. Miss Gillard was already there, gripping the lectern. The girls sat at the tables and crowded the floor, waiting for her to stop waggling her chins and tell them why they were there.

She leaned forward, staring at each of them in turn. "Girls," she began. "It's been our duty to care for you to the best of our ability while you've been here. For some of you," she nodded toward a girl called Mouse, because she'd been so small when she arrived, "it's been almost your entire lives.

"We've tried to prepare you for a world that might not always be kind to you." Miss Gillard looked over her glasses at Evie, Debby, Louise and Libby. "Some of you may not have appreciated that.

"However," she continued, "this is your last year with us. It's time for each of you to choose a career and begin training for it. I've invited some guests to talk today about careers for young women and they've very kindly agreed."

A bank manager told them about being a bank teller. A secretary talked about working in an office. The school nurse talked about nursing. One of their teachers talked about teaching.

When they were finished, Miss Gillard took the lectern again.

"You'll find some booklets about careers on the table at the back of the room. We'll put them in the library this afternoon.

Please take the time to go through them and decide what you'd like to do."

Libby whispered to Evie, "I'm just going to get married."

"You'll do no such thing!" Miss Gillard appeared out of nowhere. "Every one of my girls becomes a productive member of society when she leaves here. If you're lucky, you'll find a good husband afterward."

Evie shuffled through the booklets. She didn't want to look at money all day, or blood, or children. Being a secretary might be all right, or maybe a salesclerk. She'd always liked the idea of being a lawyer, but that was only for men. Maybe she could be a secretary in a law office. She took touch-typing and shorthand.

After Christmas, some ladies from a charity in town arrived with boxes full of donated clothing for the girls in Evie's class to wear when they were released into the outside world. Evie, pudgy from her nights in the kitchen, got a red and white polka dot dress with a white belt that didn't reach around her waist.

A few months later, a doctor talked to the girls about their bodies and showed them diagrams of what they looked like inside. He passed out slips of paper and told them to write down any questions they had. He stayed past lunchtime answering them all.

As the year went on, the outside world seemed more, not less, terrifying. One night Evie woke up in bed, sitting upright and damp with sweat. She knew what she had to do: prepare herself the best she could to survive.

She started paying attention in class and doing her homework. Louise became her only friend. At meals, she dropped as much of her food as she could inside the front of her pinafore and threw it away. No one noticed.

She tried to stop stealing food from the kitchen, but she couldn't. Instead, after shoving one or two loaves of bread into her mouth, she made herself throw up.

At first she'd squeeze into a bathroom stall and drink a mixture of vinegar and mustard, which she'd also stolen from the kitchen. After awhile all she had to do was stick her finger down her throat until she gagged. Soon all she did was take a few deep breaths until she burped a few times and she threw up right away. It burned her throat and tasted disgusting, but she was on a mission to be good enough for the outside world, and this was all part of it.

When Evie began her diet she was five feet five inches tall and weighed 165 pounds. Her weight dropped to 150, 120, and then to less than 100 pounds. She was so bony it hurt to sit down, and so weak that she had to hold onto the stair railing to drag herself upstairs.

In May, the nurse called her into the infirmary. "If you aren't going to eat on your own, I'm going to make sure you eat in here," she said.

She put Evie to bed with a glass of water and forgot about her for a day and a half. Evie was so thirsty by then that she sneaked out at lunchtime and went straight to the dining room. No one ever said anything.

By graduation day, Evie's grades were the highest in her class and she weighed 94 pounds.

She was on her way.

Chapter Two

Spring, 2001

The next Saturday morning, Kevin drives up to Sierra Fortuna from his home in Santa Barbara, an hour away.

"Kevin! Wonderful to see you, son," Nick says at the door.

"So, how are things going, Dad?"

"Just fine. I think your mother's improving, and I'm as healthy as I've always been."

"I'm glad to hear it."

"I'm just going out for my walk. I'll see you when I get back."

Kevin goes up to his room, his old room, and drops his bag on the floor. He can tell his mother has made his bed. There's no bottom sheet, but there are two pillowcases on each of the pillows.

He knocks on his parents' partly-opened door. Evie is holding a stack of scarves. She looks at him, confused.

"Hi Mom. How are you?"

She peers at him. "Who are you?"

He'd wondered if he'd feel hurt the first time she didn't recognize him, but he doesn't at all. He knew her disease would steal her memory. Why wouldn't it steal him, too?

"I'm Kevin. Your son. You know," he says, "your good child."

She breaks into a laugh of recognition.

"Kevin! Of course!" Then she looks around furtively. "Does that man know you're my son?"

"I'm pretty sure he does," Kevin says.

"Where is he?" she asks, with an intensity that surprises him.

"Out for a walk. Why?"

She leans forward. "He isn't my husband," she whispers. "I told him I'd stay here for a few days and now he won't let me go home."

"But the man who went out for a walk is your husband. His name is Nick."

"No. There's another Nick." She grasps his hand and lowers her voice even more. "We've been having an affair for years. He's supposed to come and get me, but I can't call him to tell him where I am. This man won't give me Nick's phone number. He always gives me the number of this house."

"Because this is where you and Nick live. This is your home."

She looks around in disgust. "This has never been my home," she says. "And that man is an idiot."

Kevin looks at the bedroom door just in time to see his father duck out of the doorway. "I'll be right back," Kevin says.

In his office, his father is fighting back tears.

"You know this has nothing to do with you," Kevin says.

"I know. Thanks, Kevin." He turns away. "You'd better get back to her."

Kevin sits back on the edge of his mother's bed. She looks old and sad and tired.

"I miss Nick so much, my heart hurts," she says. And then, after a moment, "He hasn't called for so long. Maybe he's telling me something."

The intensity of the pain in the house is unbearable. Kevin gives his cell phone to his father and whispers, "Call Mom on my phone. Tell her something came up at work and you can't make it back here today, but you'll call her again as soon as you can."

Kevin taps in the numbers in for him and runs back to Evie's room. "Oh Nick, I'm so glad you called," she's saying. "I want you to come and pick me up. I'm so unhappy here."

"I'll be right there. Five minutes," Nick says.

Kevin goes to his room and closes his door. Two minutes later, there's a knock. It's his father.

"She's packing," he says. "Can you do anything?"

Evie's suitcase is full. She's tying a knot in the top of her nightie.

"Can I help you fold your nightie?" Kevin asks.

"No, thank you. I'm going to put more clothes in here. I didn't realize I had so many clothes in this house." She starts stuffing blouses into her nightie.

The doorbell rings. Kevin looks over the stair railing and in Nick walks. He's put on his red baseball cap. Evie is already halfway down the stairs.

"Hi Evie, it's me, Nick."

Evie runs to him. He leads her to the love seat and puts his arm around her shoulders. She leans against him. They talk softly. Kevin hears him laugh.

They climb the stairs together. At the top, Nick gives Kevin a wink. "We're going to have a nap."

An hour later, they come out of their room. Evie looks furious.

Aiden offers to sleep at her grandparents' house during the week.

"You're too young to do that," Kathy protests.

"I want to," Aiden says. "Grandpa needs me."

Her grandfather tells her the same thing when she arrives that afternoon with her floppy-eared little dog.

"We'll be fine," he says. "You should be going out with your friends."

"I see them at school. I want to be with you and Grandma now."

She helps buy groceries, cooks meals, makes sure both her grandparents take their medications. When she catches Evie squeezing insecticide into the sink instead of dish detergent, she starts doing the dishes.

Aiden picks Kathy up at the airport. "You've gotten so thin," Kathy says on the drive back to Nick and Evie's. "Are you eating enough?"

Aiden gives her a sideways nod. "Yeah," she says, "but it's getting hard to go to school when Grandma and Grandpa need me so much. I don't think Grandpa understands what's going on."

She sighs. "I don't understand, either. I try to imagine how Grandma thinks and I just can't do it. Sometimes I see her looking for the date in the newspaper, so she can pretend she knows what day it is. The next minute she makes complete sense, like one thought can just cut through all the tangles in her brain."

Kathy puts her hand on Aiden's knee. "Thanks for everything you're doing, honey," she says. "Uncle Kevin and I will figure something else out."

That evening, an old friend of Nick and Evie calls to say he'll be passing by Sierra Fortuna on his way up the coast in a couple of days and asks if he can drop in for lunch.

"Any time, Fred," Nick booms into the phone. "We'd both love to see you." He whistles for the rest of the day.

When Kathy goes downstairs the next morning, Evie is fumbling with last night's roast chicken.

"Morning, Mom," Kathy says. "What are you doing?"

"Making chicken salad. Uncle Fred's coming for lunch today. Who else is coming, do you know?"

"Just Uncle Fred," Kathy says. "But he won't be here until tomorrow."

That afternoon, Kathy finds her mother in the kitchen again. This time, Evie is putting all the food from the fridge onto the counter.

"How many people are coming for dinner again?" she asks Kathy. "I hope we have enough to eat."

"This is plenty, Mom. It's only Uncle Fred, and he's coming for lunch tomorrow."

The next morning, Nick comes into the kitchen, whistling again. "Are you ready for our visitor today?" he asks, rubbing his hands together.

"Is someone coming?" Evie asks.

The phone rings and he reaches over to answer it. "Well, good morning, Fred, old man," he says. "We're looking forward to seeing you.... Yes, that's just—"

Evie leaps up and grabs the phone. "Fred! That isn't Nick! He's just pretending he is! You have to call Nick right now and tell him to come and get me!"

"Evie?" Kathy and Nick hear Fred say.

"Call the police!" Evie cries. "He kidnapped me!"

Nick grabs the phone back. "Fred. It's Nick. I'm so sorry." His voice cracks. "Evie gets confused sometimes. We're both looking forward to seeing you."

Ten minutes later, the phone rings again.

"Uh huh," Nick says, and then, "I'm sorry, Fred. I hope you feel better soon."

Evie goes to bed. Nick goes up to his office.

"Dad," Kathy says, "this is too much. Kevin and I'll find a caregiver to help you with Mom."

"Absolutely not," Nick says. "Your mother gets a little temperamental sometimes, but she always comes around. We're just fine."

He leans toward her, his chin jutting out. "Besides," he says, "I won't have a stranger in the house. What would she do? Tell me what she could do that we can't do for ourselves."

"She could take you grocery shopping, make dinner for you and clean up after. Most of all she'd be around to make sure Mom is safe, especially in the evenings."

"Safe?" he explodes. "You don't think I can keep your mother safe? We don't need anyone but Aiden, and that's that."

The next day, Aiden drives Kathy back to the airport.

"I had no idea it was so bad," Kathy said. "They definitely need a caregiver. It's far too much for you."

This time Aiden doesn't argue. She hasn't told her mother the worst of it.

Afternoons and evenings, especially, Evie gets desperate to go home to her husband. First, she asks Nick to call the real Nick and ask him to come and get her, but this Nick always says he can't do it. Then she tells him to call their children so they can call the real Nick. He does, his voice breaking.

The real Nick never comes. Evie sits stiffly in her chair until he tells her it's time for bed.

"I'm not going to bed with YOU," she says.

At night, Nick wakes up, and sometimes she isn't beside him in their bed, the one they've shared for forty-six years. If she isn't in one of the other bedrooms, he panics. Pain shoots through his left knee as he makes his way down the stairs to look for her.

Usually she goes down the street, to Brett's house, and asks him to call Nick. Sometimes she goes to the houses of other neighbors she knows, thinking he's there. Sometimes she goes to the houses of neighbors she doesn't know at all. They all know her, though.

Almost everyone in the neighborhood has seen Evie walking with their old dog, Gracie. They used to walk along the green-shaded sidewalks to the top of Quail Hill. Gracie would lie at Evie's feet while Evie watched the sun break into its full yellow-red glory from behind the mountains to the east. They usually took the long way home and watched the preschoolers playing at the park. They met mothers and children walking to school and neighbors working in their gardens. Gracie loved them all.

Now, when Evie rings neighbors' doorbells and pounds on their doors in the middle of the night, they know to call Nick. By the time he arrives, she usually goes with him willingly. She falls asleep as soon as she lies down in bed, but he stays wide awake for the rest of the night.

One night, Evie makes it all the way to the freeway and stands at the on ramp in her nightie. The highway patrol drives her home.

As the weeks pass, she becomes terrified of this man who calls himself her husband. One night she can't remember how to open the front door to escape from him. She's so desperate that she sleeps in the garage, huddled in the back seat of the car. Sometimes, she scratches and punches him.

Once she attacks him with a pencil. "I'll kill you if you touch me," she says.

1948

Evie left the Girls' Home three years after the war ended. She was on the front steps watching for her parents, but she didn't recognize her father getting out of the new green Ford and limping toward her. He was still tall and handsome, but he looked skinny. One of his shirtsleeves was pinned to his shoulder.

She knew her mother, though, even after all those years, and ran to her instinctively, wildly. She stumbled on the driveway and fell at their feet.

"Darling!" Her mother knelt down and swept her into her arms.

The feeling was almost painful. Evie felt bones and angles in her mother's body that she didn't fit anymore. Or maybe they were bones and angles in her own body that didn't fit her mother's.

Her father had bent down and was sweeping the gravel from her knees with his right hand. She hadn't remembered that his eyes were so beautiful, green with flecks of gold. And they were kind, and deep, and she fell in love with him.

"Look Mother," he said as they walked to the car. "Our little Evie is all grown up. She's taller than you."

Evie saw her mother looking at her as she sat between her parents in the front seat. "You have such a pretty face," her mother said. "But you're so thin. Haven't you been eating?"

"Never mind, Mother," her father said. "Your cooking will put some meat on her bones soon enough."

Evie closed her eyes. Moments later, she was leaning against her mother, asleep.

She woke up when the car turned into the driveway. Ahead was a two-story Spanish-style house, with white stucco walls and deep blue trim, a red tile roof, a long, wide front porch and an arched doorway. It looked like a house in a dream Evie used to have.

The living room was dark, with walnut floors and doors and heavy curtains pulled against the sun. Evie's father carried her suitcase up the stairs to a room, her room, with a twin bed, a bureau and a rocking chair, all white. White frilly curtains, pale pink walls. A white bedspread with small pink flowers embroidered on it. A ballerina lamp on the white bedside table.

Evie's mother followed her into the room. "It's just the same as when you left," she said. "Do you remember it?"

It was worse than landing in the jungle, or on Mars, or even in the Girls' Home, because at least there no one would expect her to feel as if she belonged. But these strangers were her parents, and this strange house and this strange room were her home.

And still her mother was watching her, waiting for her to look pleased, to say something, anything, after all this time.

Her mother tried to make up for the missing years. She drove Evie into town and bought her clothes at the Ladies' Shoppe on Main Street. Sometimes they ate lunch at the counter of the five and dime. Now that Evie was away from the Girls' Home, she was gaining weight.

"I'm so glad you're here, Evie," her mother said in a rush of breath one day. "We missed you so much."

"Then why didn't you come for me sooner?"

Evie hadn't meant it as an accusation, but her mother flinched. She grabbed the bill and stalked to the front counter to pay. Evie followed, ashamed. As soon as they got home, her mother went to her room and closed her door.

Later that afternoon, her father knocked on her door. He sat on the edge of her bed. "Your mother is very upset," he said. "I'm sure you didn't mean to hurt her feelings, but I'd like you to apologize to her."

Evie hung her head. "Okay."

But it wasn't fair and Evie knew it.

Her father held out his hand to her. "Come on," he said. "Let's go downstairs."

Evie began avoiding her mother, but she loved being with her tall, golden father. She woke up early so she could have breakfast with him before he went to his office downtown, where he took care of patients every day. He would boil two three-minute eggs and she'd make the toast, buttering it evenly to every corner.

He sat at one end of the dining table and she sat on his left, next to his amputated arm. He never covered it up when he was home. Evie was fascinated by the way it ended in a stub where his elbow should have been.

"Does it hurt?" she'd asked early on.

He'd rubbed the stump with his hand.

"No," he'd said. "Do you want to feel it?"

With one finger, she'd touched the smooth, hairless skin that wrapped around the stump. It was soft and warm like hers. A thrill had gone through her. Gradually she'd stroked his arm, over the bumpy seam, brushing against the fine, golden hairs, up to his shoulder and back down, over the seam to the smooth, hairless skin again.

Her father had looked at her. "By my age, everyone is wounded," he'd said. "Some wounds you can see, and some you can't. The ones you can't see are almost always the ones that hurt the most."

Sometimes they sat quietly reading the newspaper. Sometimes he talked to her about something he'd read. Sometimes he asked her about herself.

"Are you going out with your friends today?" he'd ask, or, "There's a good movie playing in town. Why don't you ask some of your friends if they want to see it with you? I can drive you."

Evie wondered what made him think she had any friends.

After her father went to work, Evie read the help wanted ads. Mariposa was a market town, about halfway between Los Angeles and San Francisco and halfway between the ocean and the mountains. It was beautiful, but it didn't have many secretarial jobs.

Soon she found a job as a receptionist at a legal office in Sierra Fortuna, a university town about half an hour bus ride to the west.

"Are you sure you want to work so far away?" both her parents asked. "Why don't you just stay here and take it easy for the rest of the summer? You can decide what you want to do later on."

They seemed more attached to her than she'd realized, but she felt nothing but relief that she was getting away. Even from her kind, gentle father.

Evie was proud of her job, greeting clients and fielding phone calls for Mr. Burbank, a divorce lawyer. The marriage boom had begun after the war and the boom in divorces was just starting. Sheila, his legal secretary, was one of the first people to welcome her.

Evie was almost speechless when Sheila walked up to her. Her shiny black hair was styled like photos she'd seen of movie stars, sultry and falling below her shoulders. She was wearing a straight black skirt that just covered her knees and a silky blouse cinched into the belt at her small waist. She had an open, white smile and wore bright red lipstick. She was beautiful.

Sheila taught her how to file, and when Sheila was busy Evie did the filing for her. Eventually, Sheila taught her everything a legal secretary had to know, from where to find the information Mr. Burbank needed for his cases to how to prepare documents for court.

One day, Sheila went up to Evie at the reception desk.

"Hi Evie," Sheila smiled. "I like your outfit."

Evie blushed. She was wearing a straight black skirt that just covered her knees and a silky blouse tucked into a belt, which she'd bought with her first paycheck. It didn't look the same on her as it did on Sheila, though.

"It looks a lot like one I have."

"It does?"

"Yes," Sheila said.

"Oh."

"I saw some clothes in a shop the other day that I think would look nice on you. Would you like me to take you there at lunchtime?"

"Oh, yes. Thank you!"

Sheila was silent.

"I'm sorry I copied you."

"That's all right," Sheila said. "You won't have to anymore."

At the shop, Sheila went straight to a rack of skirts and pulled out a lavender, pink and blue one that flared from the waist to the hem. She moved to another rack and examined a blue jacket with a narrow waist and oversized shoulder pads.

"Hmmm. Take a look at these."

She held them up against Evie. "You look better in lighter colors because of your light skin," she said. "You can wear them with this blouse, or just the skirt with this pink angora sweater."

"Gosh, Sheila...."

Sheila hung them over Evie's arm. "Come over here."

She led Evie to the lingerie section. A saleslady pulled out a few bras with wrinkled white cotton cups and one with cones that pointed straight ahead.

Evie blushed. "Sheila. I could never...."

Sheila hung them over the sweater. The cones jutted toward the ceiling.

"Just try them on and show me what they look like," she said. "Do you have any tissues?"

"No. Wh—"

"I'll bring a box," the saleslady told Sheila.

She pressed Evie's back. "Come with me, dear. We'll find you a dressing room."

The saleslady put a tissue inside the cups of the pointy bra to fill it out. Evie was still blushing when Sheila knocked on the door and handed her a girdle.

"Try this on, too," Sheila said. "It'll make your tummy flatter."

Evie let it hang from her fingers, a wide elastic panel with four lengths of elastic with a hook dangling from each one. She pulled, tugged, wriggled it on. It felt strangely comforting, as if it were hugging her lower body.

She slipped on the pointy bra and adjusted the tissues, and pulled on the skirt and sweater. She almost laughed when she saw herself in the mirror.

"Is your sweater from Egypt?" the girls at the Home used to ask each other.

"No."

"Then why does it have two pyramids in front?"

Ha ha ha.

She tore off everything and put on the smallest bra with the blouse and skirt. She smiled in surprise. Maybe she was a little bit pretty.

Another knock on the door. "How are you doing in there?"

Evie opened the door and let Sheila and the saleslady examine her.

"Stand straight," Sheila commanded.

She turned to the saleslady. "She'll take everything."

On the way back to work, Sheila didn't stop talking.

"When you get your next paycheck, buy a pearl necklace and a few sets of earrings. Start with pearls. You need pumps with low heels to match your outfit. Maybe a scarf or two. Lipstick and rouge. I'll help you pick the shades. And, of course, white gloves. You can buy them as you have more money. I'll give you my hairdresser's phone number. She can probably do something with your hair."

Sheila taught her how to pluck her eyebrows, and how to put on rouge to emphasize her cheekbones and lipstick to make her lips look full. Her hairdresser gave her a shoulder-length hairstyle that flipped out at the ends. Evie slept on pink curlers with bristles that poked into her head all night to make her hair puff out. Her hairstyle drew attention to her face, which really did look pretty now.

The first morning Evie did her hair and put on makeup, her father looked up from the breakfast table in surprise.

"Who's this?" he asked. "My little girl is growing up."

"You look beautiful, Evie," her mother said, "but are you sure you want to look so sophisticated at your age?"

Evie didn't say what she was thinking. "Of course."

Of course, indeed. Clients and lawyers visiting Mr. Burbank began lingering at the reception desk. They joked with her and complimented her, and she learned to joke back. Especially when they asked her out.

"Why don't you want to go out with any of them?" Sheila asked.

"I'm not ready," Evie said. "I just started working."

"If you get married you won't have to work," Sheila said. "That's the whole point of looking attractive. Trust me, some of the men around here would make very good husband material."

One day, Sheila asked Evie if she'd like to share Sheila's apartment.

"You've only known this girl for a few months," her father said. "You may not know what she's really like."

"What if she invites men back to the apartment?" her mother asked. "Have you met any of her friends?"

Evie knew what they were really saying. "We love you. We don't want you to leave us."

It felt wrong to care so little about her parents' feelings, but Evie didn't have time to think about that. "Thanks, Mom, Dad, but I already told her I would. I'll come back and see you whenever I can."

Evie didn't expect that to be very often.

Her parents drove her to Sheila's apartment. Evie and her father each lugged a suitcase up the three flights of stairs. Sheila was on a date, so Evie showed them through the living room to the small kitchen, the bathroom and the bedroom. She poured three glasses of lemonade and they sat on the sofa in the living room.

"It's quite nice," her mother said in the silence.

"Yes," her father added a moment later. "I'm sure you'll be happy here."

Evie walked down the stairs and back to the car with them.

"We'll miss you, Evie," her mother said.

"Come and see us old folks whenever you can." Her father's eyes were glistening.

Evie waved goodbye. She hopped back up the stairs before they were out of sight.

Evie was still unpacking when Sheila got back home. Her hair was slipping free of its bobby pins and her lipstick was smudged.

"You aren't going to wear THAT again," Sheila said as Evie pulled out the gray suit her mother had bought her during one of their shopping trips.

"I know it's plain, but...."

Sheila pulled the rest of Evie's clothes out of the suitcases and threw them into two piles on the bed. "You can keep the clothes in this pile, but you have to get rid of those," she said. "I'll take you shopping again. And where are your date clothes?"

"Date clothes?"

"You know. Clothes you wear on a date."

"I've never...."

"Never?"

"I'd never even talked to a man except my father before I started working at the office."

Sheila stared at her.

"When could I have?"

Sheila flounced down on the bed. "Oh, Evie. Do you ever have some catching up to do. It can take years to meet the right man, and you have to be ready. And that means makeup, and a nice hairdo and sexy clothes. All the time."

"Sheila?"

"Mm hmm?"

"Have you ever...you know?"

Sheila's eyes narrowed. "You know?"

"Yeah. You know."

She nodded. "Yes. Why?

"Because I really want to."

"Well, then, start getting ready now. You have to meet a lot of men before you find one to get serious with. You can be attracted to someone who seems to have a great future, and not find out till it's too late that he's a jerk or a liar or worse."

"Did that happen to you?"

"All I'm saying is you have to be careful. It's too easy to get into real trouble if you pick the wrong man."

Sheila stood up and took off her earrings and bracelet and shook her hair free of the last bobby pins. She stepped out of her dress and slip and turned on the shower.

Evie followed her into the bathroom. Sheila's cosmetics spilled across the counter like a treasure trove: gold tubes of bright red lipsticks and dark mascara, silver cases of eye shadows, shiny bottles of nail polish.

"So how was your date?"

"He's a two. He works at a good law firm, but he has clammy hands."

"Ah."

"I liked Tom from last night better. He's studying to be a chartered accountant, but I'd much rather date someone who already has a good job."

"Uh huh."

"Why did you say "Uh huh," like that?"

"I don't know. I just don't think I could think about men that way."

"It's a dog eat dog world." Sheila tested the water with her hand. "The war vets are getting snapped up as fast as they graduate from university. It won't be long before they're all taken. So do you want to go shopping on Saturday?"

"I guess so. Thanks, Sheila."

Sheila stepped into the shower. "It'll have to be in the afternoon. I have a big date with a guy in medical school on Friday night."

Sheila went back to Chicago to spend the Christmas holidays with her parents. Evie's parents had asked her to go home, but she'd said no. She still didn't understand why she felt such pain when she saw them.

She looked around her apartment. "This is my home," she thought.

On the morning before Christmas, Evie wandered along a path beside the creek. Iridescent raindrops hung from the dried-out stalks of the summer's wildflowers, and water skimmed over the stones in a rush of white bubbles. She stopped to watch the last leaves of the year drift by, and then continued along the path to the mission.

White walls of the mission enclosed the courtyard. Along the gravel path to the rose garden, the air teemed with the scent of lavender and the hum of honeybees. Evie paused under a heavy wooden arbor collapsing under the weight of an ancient grapevine and let the sharp wine scent of the fallen fruit fill her nostrils.

She followed the path to a bench and sat facing a small pond. Bubbles popped in the silent water, and two giant koi slid toward her, their mouths gaping hopefully. She closed her eyes and let the sun wash over her. The smells of fruit and flowers from figs, pomegranates, oranges, lemons and olives filled the air. Somewhere a generator was humming. She was so at peace, she felt like crying.

Footsteps crunched on the path, and just as she opened her eyes, a young man stopped in front of her. He was tall and handsome, with a long face and thin blond hair. For a moment, with the sunlight behind him, she thought he was her father. When she realized he wasn't, her heartbeat quickened and she felt herself blush.

"'Morning," he said. "It's a beautiful day to get some sun, isn't it?"

Evie tried to speak in her normal voice. "Yes."

"My name's Ted. Mind if I sit down?"

She slid over.

Ted told Evie that he was an architecture student at the university and he liked coming to the mission for inspiration. The modern building style was going to be geometrics and glass, he said, but that wasn't for him, and there would always be a market for buildings that were classically beautiful.

He leaned toward her. "So, what about you? Do you live around here?"

Evie told him about her job in Sierra Fortuna and her parents back in Mariposa.

"You aren't spending Christmas all by yourself, are you?"

"Yes," she said, "I really wanted to stay here."

"Well, you can't spend it alone. Why don't you come to my apartment tomorrow and we can have Christmas dinner together?"

Evie couldn't believe it. No makeup, no hairdo, no sexy clothes. He liked her the way she was, and he was going to be an architect. Well, why shouldn't she have beginner's luck?

He bought her a hamburger at a restaurant across from the mission and ordered them both a beer. Her heart began thumping in a strange pattern: excitement, doom, excitement, doom. She waited for one to win out over the other but it was a tie, until the waitress put the bottles and the mugs on the table and Ted poured the golden liquid into hers.

He looked at her with a crooked grin. "Well? You aren't going to hurt my feelings and not drink up, are you?"

Evie picked up the mug, cold, wet and heavy. Touched it to her lips and felt the froth, tasted the bitterness as it slid down her throat.

He laughed. "It isn't that bad, is it? Try again. You'll get used to it."

She was beginning to feel something that made drinking it worthwhile: a warm, tingling that spread down her arms and legs and calmed the pounding of her heart. She put her mug down and smiled.

"That's better. Bottoms up." Ted tipped his mug until it was empty and banged it down onto the table. "Come on, have a bite of your hamburger before we go."

Evie stumbled as she stood up. Disconcerted, she grabbed onto the back of her chair for support.

"Whoa, there." As Ted caught her arm, she thought she saw a glimmer in his eyes. She shook his hand away.

"What's the matter?" He looked genuinely hurt. Maybe she'd been mistaken.

"Come here." He pointed to a bench just outside the restaurant. "Sit here with me for a minute."

He looked into her eyes. "I'm sorry if I upset you," he said. "Forgive me?" He smiled again. "Please? I don't want you to be mad at me."

She found herself smiling back. The glow inside her was dampening the spark of fear. In fact, it was spreading to other parts of her body and they were signaling her to stay with him, no matter what.

"I'm not mad at you." She put her hand on his thigh, surprised at how natural it felt.

He swallowed. "Why don't I show you my apartment now, so you'll be able to find it easily tomorrow?"

It was only a couple of blocks away and very easy to find, but Evie didn't say anything. Instead, as if she were one of the leaves in the creek, she let herself trail behind him, up the stairs to his apartment on the third floor and straight into his bedroom.

When he kissed her, everything fell away except her need to keep the connection alive. His hands exploring her body became her world. But when he began to unbutton her blouse, she backed away.

"Trust me," he murmured. "I won't do anything you don't want me to do."

She surrendered. And when she felt his bare chest against her breasts, she almost collapsed with the pleasure. They spent the next three days together, most of it in bed. They ate peanut butter sandwiches and drank beer; just enough to keep the buzz going, Ted said.

Evie couldn't decide if the haze she was in was because of the beer or because of the way she felt being in bed with him. Even when they weren't making love, they were touching, always touching. She couldn't get enough of being skin to skin, and when he was inside her, of the sensation that they were sealed together forever.

Now she knew what love felt like.

But as they sprawled in the rumpled sheets on the morning of the fourth day, he said, "Evie, this has been great, but you have to go now."

She laughed. "Where?"

"Back to your place."

At first time stopped. Then it began swirling. She took a breath. "What do you mean?"

"I know I should have told you before. My girlfriend's coming back this afternoon."

Evie froze. He was done with her, that easily. She'd been completely caught up in her feelings and he'd just been passing the time till his girlfriend got home. Oh god. She clung to the sheet as she picked up her clothes and went into the bathroom to get dressed. She gathered her things from the counter and stuffed them into her bag. She thought he looked slightly guilty as he sat on the edge of the bed.

He held out his hand to her. "We've had fun. Haven't we?"

She brushed past him.

"Don't be like that."

"Don't you dare talk to me."

She walked out with her back straight. When she got back to her apartment, Sheila was there.

"Where've you been? What's wrong?"

She told Sheila everything.

"Evie. I'll spare you the lecture," Sheila said. "But I don't care how you feel about a man you just met, you do not go straight to bed with him. And you never, ever, drink with a stranger. Have you got that?"

Evie spent the rest of the night crying. She remembered the feeling she'd had years ago at the Girls' Home after she'd played jelly belly with the other girls. It was shame.

Shame swept through her again.

Chapter Three

Summer, 2001

A little more than a week after Kathy returns home from seeing her parents, her phone rings. She can barely make out her mother's voice.

"Kathy? Is that you?"

"Yes, Mom. Are you okay?"

"I think I did something very bad today." Evie's voice becomes garbled and Aiden comes on the line.

"Mom? We had a little excitement here this morning. Grandma called 911 and told the dispatcher that Grandpa had a gun and was holding her hostage. An entire SWAT team showed up. Luckily they saw my phone number on the fridge and called me. They were going to evacuate everyone on the street until I finally convinced them what was going on."

Kathy can hear Evie in the background. "I know I'm causing everyone so much trouble," she says.

"You aren't causing any trouble, Grandma," Aiden tells her. "Why don't you go and brush your teeth?" And a moment later, "I'll help you find it in a minute."

Aiden speaks back into the phone. "I love Grandma and Grandpa," she says, "but things are getting worse here and I don't think I can help enough. The blood vessels in Grandpa's eyes are starting to pop out from the pressure."

Aiden notices that some of the scratches on Nick's arm are infected and makes an appointment to see Dr. Fletcher on a Friday afternoon. The doctor examines Nick's arm. Without expression, he examines his other one.

"Where did you get all these scratches and bruises?"

Silence.

"Nick?"

"She doesn't mean to do it," he says. "Sometimes she just gets angry for a few minutes."

Dr. Fletcher turns to Evie.

"Evie?"

"He isn't my husband," Evie says. "He won't let me call Nick and tell him where I am."

The doctor's eyes widen. "Who are you again?" he asks Aiden.

"Their granddaughter."

Dr. Fletcher picks up Evie's folder and starts flipping through it. "There's a report in here from a psychiatrist at the hospital. She thinks Evie has dementia." He pauses. "Possibly Alzheimer's disease."

"That's ridiculous," Nick scoffs. "There's nothing wrong with her. I'd know if there was."

The doctor looks up at Nick. "The psychiatrist didn't mention it to you?"

"Of course not," Nick lies.

Dr. Fletcher looks back at Aiden. "Are you staying with them?"

"At night, yes."

"How often does this happen?"

"Only when Grandma doesn't recognize Grandpa," Aiden says.

"And how often is that?"

She squirms. "About three times a week."

Dr. Fletcher looks at her under his shaggy white eyebrows. "Does someone else stay with them when you aren't there?"

"No."

The doctor leans against his bookcase and crosses his arms.

"Nick," he says at last. "You can't deny that Evie has a problem. And if it's Alzheimer's disease, which I suspect it might be, it won't be long before she needs much more care than you and Aiden can give her. I want you to bring her back here next week and I'll do some tests. They won't be definitive, but they'll give us a good idea of where things stand."

"Of course," Nick says. "But it'll be a waste of time. She's just fine."

"Yes, well, in the meantime, I'll send a prescription to your pharmacy for something that should help calm her down in the evenings. And here are some pamphlets for you to look through."

In the car, Evie sifts through the pamphlets, for caregiver agencies, the Alzheimer's Association, medic-alert bracelets, nursing homes and door alarm systems.

"But these are for old people," she says.

Aiden calls her mother as soon as they get home. Kathy calls Kevin.

"I talked to him about a caregiver and he still refuses to discuss it," Kevin says, "but if she's hitting and scratching him we have to do something soon."

"What about Sunset Acres?"

"He'd never agree to being apart from her," Kevin says. "They're like swans. They've mated for life."

"Sunset Acres is a nice place," Kathy says. "And it's close to them, so he could visit whenever he wanted to."

"That's where they put Grandma Landry when she had Alzheimer's. They both think of it as a place full of old people strapped into their wheelchairs, with their heads sagging onto their chests."

"Still, they didn't have a problem putting her there. Why would it be so awful to do it to Mom?"

"That was different. Grandma Landry didn't have a husband."

"Maybe it wouldn't be that bad," Kathy says. "Mom is always saying she doesn't live at their house, so in her mind that isn't even her home anymore. And they could see each other as often as they wanted."

Kevin looks at her. "I know you and Mom haven't always gotten along. That isn't affecting what you want to do, is it?"

"Of course not. I feel sorry for both of them."

"You know what the irony is," Kevin says. "Mom has dreaded this disease ever since she saw what it did to Grandma Landry. She always told us she didn't want to live if it happened to her. But now she's just accepting it."

The next week, Aiden drives Evie and Nick to the appointment with Dr. Fletcher. They make small talk, until Nick notices that Dr. Fletcher is taking notes. He stiffens and realizes that the doctor is doing what Nick used to do with new clients: Put them at ease so he could assess them without their noticing it.

Dr. Fletcher hands Evie a few papers that look like a child's homework. She can't recognize an elephant or copy a circle.

"Evie," Dr. Fletcher asks, "do you know where you live?"

"She lives in Sierra Fortuna with me," Nick replies.

"Evie?"

"I live in two houses," she says. "They look exactly the same."

"Two houses? Why?"

"I live in one house with my husband, Nick, but this man is making me stay in his house."

Nick looks away.

Dr. Fletcher takes a deep breath. "I'm sorry to tell you, Evie, but you may well have Alzheimer's disease. I strongly advise you and Nick to contact the Alzheimer's Association as soon as possible. They're compassionate, knowledgeable people and they'll be able to guide you through the challenges you're going to have to face."

As they leave the office, Evie grips Nick's arm. "What did I say?"

"Nothing," Nick says. But his lips stay in a tight line for the rest of the way home.

A week later, Kathy flies in to take her parents for a tour of Sunset Acres. She isn't even sitting down before Evie leans forward and puts her hand on hers.

"Kathy?" she says. "Are you Kathy?"

"Yes, Mom. I'm Kathy."

"There's something I have to tell someone." Evie stops. "I remember you from the Home. You were always nice. Are you sure you're Kathy?"

"Yes, I am."

Evie gathers her strength. "I've been having an affair, for years. I feel so guilty."

"You have?"

"It's with a man I've known for a long time. His name is Nick. Dad would be so hurt if he knew."

"I think Dad would understand."

Evie's entire body relaxes. "You do?"

"Yes, Mom. I do. You don't have to worry about it anymore."

Nick comes into the room. "I heard my name. Have you been talking about me?"

"Of course, dear," Evie says, turning in her chair and smiling at him. "What else would we ever talk about?"

He kisses her on the cheek.

"Are you almost ready for the tour of Sunset Acres?" Kathy asks.

Nick pulls away. "Not if anyone is going to try to talk me into putting your mother in there."

"No, Dad. We're just going to take a look."

The three of them have barely sat down with the counselor when Nick leans toward her. "Before we go any further, I want to make sure you understand that if my wife moves here, I'll be moving in with her," he says.

The counselor and Kathy look at each other. "I'm afraid I can't guarantee that, Nick. Your needs," the counselor chooses her words carefully, "are different than Evie's. You wouldn't be qualified to go into a nursing home."

He leans forward, aggressively this time. "How are my needs different? Tell me that."

"The only problem you have is with your memory," Kathy says.

"There's nothing wrong with my memory," he practically spits. "I can still remember every single person in my graduating class in high school."

"Then you don't need special care at all," Kathy points out.

Nick stands up. "A nursing home for my wife is out of the question. I won't allow us to be separated."

The counselor looks at Kathy. Kathy shakes her head.

"Of course," the counselor says. "If you change your mind, please let me know."

As soon as they arrive home, Evie turns on them both. "I'd like to know why no one asked me what I want to do," she snaps.

"You're right, Mom," Kathy says. "What do you want to do?"

"I want to stay here. I've lived in this house for almost fifty years. My friends are here. I know all my neighbors. I can look out the living room window and watch children playing. I'd rather close the garage door and turn on the car engine than spend the rest of my life surrounded by a bunch of old people."

"Mom, you don't mean that!"

"I mean it with all my heart. I know I'm old," she goes on, "and I might be forgetful sometimes. But I haven't lost all my marbles yet. I wish everyone would give me some credit for knowing what's best for myself. I know what I'm capable of, and what I'm not. All I need is a little help sometimes, that's all."

Later, when Evie and Nick are in bed, Nick envelopes her in a hug.

"I'm so scared, Nick."

"I'll never let them take you away. You know that."

"That isn't it. I know something is happening to me, but I don't understand what. Things get mixed up in my brain." Tears well up in her eyes. "I know I'm a lot of trouble for you these days. I'm so sorry."

"You've always been trouble." He kisses her forehead. "But I'll keep you anyway."

1949

Ten weeks after Evie's encounter with Ted, Sheila took her to a medical student she knew for the abortion. Evie felt nothing at the thought of losing this piece of tissue growing like a tumor inside her. There was no room in her heart for more pain.

Sheila tucked her into bed afterward. She smoothed Evie's hair and leaned over to kiss her cheek. "Go to sleep. We can talk when you feel better."

Evie closed her eyes and surrendered to the pain. The physical pain was centered in her abdomen. It took on a life of its own, expanding to fill her whole body and then receding, expanding, receding, pulsating, like a heartbeat. Soon, the pill she'd taken would soothe that.

The other pain felt like a knife stabbed and twisting in her chest, a searing pain that radiated outward. That one would take much longer to go away.

It was dark when Sheila appeared and spoon-fed Evie some soup, and it was light when she woke Evie up again. She put a tray on the table and sat on the edge of Evie's bed. Evie was still curled up facing the wall.

"Feeling better?"

"I think so."

"I'm going to work in a few minutes. I'll tell Mr. Burbank you have the flu and you probably won't be in for a few more days."

As Evie fell back into sleep, she imagined the pain as wisps that flew into the air every time she exhaled. As she inhaled, the wisps floated down and disappeared into the earth.

She woke up again early in the afternoon in the half-light of her curtained room. She ate the two slices of toast and drank the orange juice Sheila had left for her. She was still alive and she would move on. But first, she had to sleep just a little longer.

One day at work that summer, Sheila said, "Charlie from McMaster and Poore keeps asking me to talk to you. Why don't you go out with him? He's harmless."

"I don't want to go out with Charlie. I don't want to go out with anyone."

Sheila sat beside her at her desk.

"I know you're afraid, Evie, but you have to start going out into the world again. Look what happened to me."

Sheila had met her new boyfriend in Woolworth's when she was shopping for a radio. She saw him out of the corner of her eye, a slightly goofy-looking man who clomped over to her and charmed her on the spot with his smile. He won her trust by showing her a radio that was better and cost less than the one she was holding.

"If you need anything else, you know where to find me," he said with a lopsided smile as he wrapped it up for her.

Within a week, Sheila had been back for a new frying pan, dishcloths, a couple of picture frames and shoe polish.

"You really need a screwdriver?" he'd asked the last time she went in.

"Of course. How else am I going to drive...screws?"

He sighed. "I don't know how long you can keep coming in here to buy this stuff," he said, "and I'd really like to see you again. Would you like to go out with me sometime?"

"Oh, thank god. I'm just going to put this back."

"But he isn't even in university," Evie said.

"I know. But my plan wasn't working. Edgar is the only man I've met who I can imagine being in love with."

1950

A year later, on a breezy summer morning, Evie opened the heavy glass doors of the university's law library. She'd been passing by for almost a year but had been too intimidated to go in. All she wanted to do was take a quick look inside, she told herself.

The walnut-paneled walls stretched two floors to the skylit ceiling and were lined with books except where stained glass windows let in glints of colored light. A freestanding staircase at each end of the room led up to the second floor and down to the basement, where she could glimpse more shelves of books. To her left, students at long rows of walnut tables pored over books illuminated by hanging wrought-iron lamps.

"It's quite a place, isn't it?"

The young man collecting books piled at the end of the table beside her grinned up at her. His curly black hair was slightly too long for him to look like a serious student, Evie thought, and his quick smile didn't look like the smile of any lawyer she'd ever seen.

"I've never been in here before," she admitted. "Do you know where I can find books about family law?"

"Sure. In the basement, over against the far wall." He looked as if he wanted to say more, but she cut him off.

"Thank you."

Evie loved it in the basement, cushioned in an armchair, surrounded by thousands of leather-bound books with gilt edges, and the scent of lemon furniture polish, dust and what the future might offer her.

On Christmas morning, Evie, Sheila and Edgar sat around the tree that Evie and Sheila had carried home from the lot down the street, drinking coffee and opening the presents they'd given each other. Edgar gave Sheila a large box that he'd wrapped himself. Inside was a smaller one, and inside that was a smaller one still. When Sheila opened the last, tiny box, a diamond ring sparkled in its cushion of black velvet.

Edgar got down on one knee. "I love you, Sheila. Will you marry me?"

Sheila fell to her knees and hugged him. "What took you so long?" she asked. A moment later, she was in tears

1951

Evie would have kept going to the library if Charlie, the lawyer from McMaster and Poore who was still hanging around the reception desk, hadn't asked her out to dinner again.

"It's Valentine's Day next Wednesday," he said. "You don't want to be sitting at home all by yourself, do you?"

He picked her up in his red convertible.

"Wow. This is really something," Evie said, stroking the soft black leather on the bucket seats.

He grinned. "We can go for a drive after dinner if you want."

She shook her head. "Maybe."

He laughed. "Maybe not, then. Want the top up?"

"No, thanks." Evie wrapped Sheila's scarf around her hair and tied it under her chin.

Charlie drove with his right hand loosely on the steering wheel, his left elbow on the window frame and his body leaning back into the soft leather seat. He had a comforting masculinity that Evie hadn't noticed before.

"Enjoying yourself?" he asked.

"Yes. I am."

"You sound surprised."

"I guess I am. I never pictured myself in a car like this. I almost feel glamorous."

He glanced at her. "Almost? Then you have no idea how beautiful you are, Evelyn Madison."

He swung into a parking space at the restaurant, jumped out of the car and opened her car door for her. Before she could catch her breath, he produced a bouquet of red roses from the back seat.

"Charlie. Thank you."

"You have a few hairs out of place," he said, and he brushed her cheek with his fingers.

"Much better," he murmured.

She felt the urge again, all evening, but after dinner she asked him to drive her home.

They dated for months. At first, every time they held hands, every time they kissed, every time he held her face in his palms and looked into her eyes, she wanted to fall into bed with him. As time went on, though, it became easier to resist the urge. And easier.

"I don't feel the same way about him as I used to," Evie told Sheila. "He's started telling me what to wear. The other day, he ordered for me when we were out for dinner, without even asking me what I wanted. He says he knows what's best for me."

Sheila put her hand on Evie's arm.

"I can tell by the way he looks at you that he loves you," Sheila said. "Isn't that what you want?" But she didn't sound very sure.

On their six-month anniversary, Charlie took Evie back to the restaurant where they'd gone on their first date. He held her hands across the table.

"I hope you know I'm in love with you," he said.

"I love you, too," Evie lied.

"I got a promotion last week."

"That's wonderful. Congratulations, Charlie."

"It means I'll be able to start a family."

He reached into his pocket. She watched him take out a small jewelry box and flip open the lid.

A diamond ring, as cold as ice.

"You said no?" Sheila asked. "He's a lawyer, he's good-looking and he's in love with you. Do you know how long it could take before you meet someone else like him?"

"He's always telling me what to do. I don't think that's love."

"Evie...."

"I want to be like you and Edgar. You're so in love with each other, it makes me feel like crying."

"Not everybody is lucky enough to have what Edgar and I have. I'm not saying you should worry, but how many more available men do you think are out there? You aren't getting any younger, you know."

And what was Evie thinking, that such love could ever come to her?

Sheila and Edgar were married that December, almost a year after they became engaged. Evie was the maid of honor. After the reception, with the food and the drinks and the dancing, she took a taxi back to her apartment.

Crumpled boxes sprawled across the living room floor. Dishes of limp salad and pasta drying at the edges spilled across the kitchen counters. Piles of clothing covered the beds.

Evie missed Sheila already. But now that Sheila wasn't there to bully her into dating, she started spending her spare time in the law library again. Sometimes she saw the dark-haired young man shelving the books. Whenever he shyly said hello to her, she gave him a quick smile and looked away.

1952

One spring evening, Evie received a phone call from her father.

"Can you come home?" he asked. "Your mother's taken a turn for the worse."

The next Saturday morning, Evie took the bus back to see her parents. Her father met her at the door.

"Evie, darling," he said. He grasped her arm and held it for a moment. "Your mother will be so pleased to see you."

Still limping, he led her down the hallway and into their darkened bedroom. The curtains were closed, but the gloom wasn't just from the lack of sunlight. Sorrow filled the room so completely that Evie could feel it on her skin.

She looked at the bed. This couldn't be her mother, this tiny wrinkled woman snoring with her mouth open and her hands like claws on the sheet.

Evie's father touched her arm. "Mother? Evie's come to see you."

Her mother's eyes fluttered open. "Evie?" She sighed. "You're so beautiful."

"I told you she'd come," her father said. "Our Evie."

Evie sat down. Her mother looked like a prehistoric creature. All the padding under her skin was gone, and her nose, which was once small and perfect, jutted from her face like a beak. Her shoulders were as sharp and bony as a bird of prey.

Evie's father touched her shoulder. "I'll leave you together," he said.

Her mother's crabbed fingers explored her face like a blind woman's: cheeks, forehead, nose, lips, neck.

Evie thought she saw love in her mother's eyes. She almost cried with pity, not just for her, but for all three of them: the ravaged wife, the desolate husband, the daughter who so yearned to be loved.

A tear squeezed from her eyes and then another. Such a waste, Evie thought, if her mother had loved her all those years and Evie had never known.

Her mother stroked her hair, and then she pulled, and Evie realized she was trying to pull Evie toward her.

Evie's whole body resisted. "I can't even do this for her," she thought, but no tears came.

Evie's mother traced her face again, and let her hand slide down to the neck of Evie's blouse. She grabbed and pulled again, weakly, insistently, toward her. Their eyes never left each other's, never blinked.

Evie's mother lifted her hand to Evie's face again. Still looking into her eyes, she twisted Evie's nose, hard.

"Ow!" Evie pulled back and looked into her mother's eyes again. What was in there now? She couldn't tell.

She sat there, letting her mother look into her eyes. Whatever she found was up to her.

"Come into the kitchen," her father said from the doorway, and led her back down the hall. He poured her a cup of coffee, and just like she used to do, she sat beside him at the table.

He turned his cup in circles with his fingers for a moment. "Thank you for coming, my dear. I wasn't sure you would."

"Why wouldn't I?"

"I know we let you down," he said. "We are both so sorry."

Evie looked at his worn face, his gentle eyes. She could barely speak through the lump in her throat.

"Why did you go?" she asked at last.

"They needed doctors at the front," he said. "I volunteered. I knew it would be hard on your mother and you, but I couldn't stay home knowing so many boys were dying over there and I could help some of them. It seems so selfish now, putting what I wanted ahead of what was best for you two. But everyone was so sure the war would be over in a few months."

Evie watched him massage his arm. "Is it bothering you?" she asked.

"No. It's more of a habit than anything else."

"I never asked you what happened."

"A bomb, in the middle of a surgery. I was operating on a private. He'd killed his first man and he was haunted by the man's face. He deliberately fell out of a helicopter as it was taking off so he'd be injured badly enough to be sent home.

"The bomb blew in a window and part of the metal frame sliced through my arm, clean as a knife. Then the wall fell in on us. The private didn't make it."

"And then?"

"I had more than two years of surgeries and rehab, first in England and then here, but they couldn't completely repair my leg. By the time I'd recuperated enough, you were graduating from high school. We'd missed almost six years of your life."

Her father put his hand on hers. "Are you happy? Do you have a good life?"

"Yes," Evie said. "I have a good life."

"We've always loved you," he said. "You couldn't have known that."

Now there was a stinging behind Evie's eyes. "No," she said. "I didn't."

Her father stumbled to her and wrapped his arms around her. "There is so much I regret in my life," he said. "But that is by far what I regret the most."

Evie called Sheila as soon as she got back home.

"It's been months since we've seen each other," Sheila said. "I'll drop in at the office on Monday and take you out to lunch."

Sheila was as beautiful and fashionably dressed as ever, in a black and white houndstooth skirt and jacket and a dramatic black hat. Something was different, though.

"You're gaining a little weight, there," Evie said. "Marriage must suit you."

Sheila beamed.

"You aren't!"

"I am. And I'll probably throw up in the restaurant to prove it."

Evie hugged her. "I'm so happy for you. When are you due?"

"January, probably. It's sooner than we expected, but we're both thrilled. Edgar's going to make a terrific father."

"Can I be Aunt Evie?"

"Of course."

As they walked to the restaurant, Sheila asked, "So, how were your parents?"

"My mother isn't doing so well."

"Oh, I'm sorry, Evie."

"It's okay. My father's taking care of her." Her eyes teared up. "I had a good talk with him."

"Uh huh."

"He told me they were sorry about leaving me in the Home."

"Uh huh," Sheila said again.

"She twisted my nose."

"What?"

"I think she was angry because I wouldn't hug her."

"Oh, Evie."

"I just wish I knew if she loved me or not," Evie said. "You know, I almost wish she didn't. Then I wouldn't feel obligated to see her again. Does that make me a terrible person?"

Sheila shook her head. "No, it doesn't. But of course she loves you," she said. "That's why she was angry when you wouldn't hug her."

"You think so?"

"Yeah. In her own way, she does."

It was during a rare summer cloudburst that Evie noticed an orange cat staring at her from the fire escape outside her kitchen window. She huddled like a scrawny sphinx with rain dripping down her ears and face.

When Evie opened the window, the cat glared at her, flicked her tail and leaped onto the counter. In one swift motion, she sat down, raised one of her hind legs to the ceiling and began licking herself dry. When she finished, she stared at Evie again through the black slits in her green eyes.

"You sassy little cat," Evie said. She poured milk into a bowl and put it on the floor. The cat leaped down and gave it an exploratory sniff. She tucked her feet under her skinny hips, crouched forward and lapped it up.

The cat stared at her again. She turned her nose up at the bread Evie shredded for her, even when Evie soaked it in milk. Finally, Evie took two eggs from the fridge and scrambled them. The cat sniffed warily and settled herself again, taking dainty little bites until the bowl was clean.

Before Evie went to work, she closed the window until there was just enough space for the cat to slink underneath. When she got back home, Sassy was curled up on Evie's unmade bed.

No one replied to the "Found Cat" posters Evie put up, but she didn't leave them up for very long. She bought enough cat food for a few days, and when that was gone she bought more, along with bowls for food and water.

The two of them settled into a routine. When Evie arrived home from work, Sassy would slip under the kitchen window and wind herself around Evie's legs until Evie picked her up. When Evie was in the kitchen, Sassy would watch her, curled up on one of the chairs. When Evie was on the sofa, reading a magazine or watching her new TV, Sassy would leap onto her lap and fall asleep purring.

Evie hadn't realized how comforting it was to have a soft little body nestle on her lap, to knead the delicate bones under the warm fur, to feel the vibration in Sassy's throat when she purred.

Gradually Evie realized she was happy.

She was still spending Saturday afternoons in the law library. The fellow who shelved the books always happened to be there.

This Saturday, he was standing part-way down a row with a book in one hand, searching for its place on the shelf. His black hair curled over his ears and the collar of his shirt. He slipped the book into the shelf, reached into his cart for the next one and swiveled toward Evie, all in one motion. His eyes widened.

"I was just…" Evie stammered.

He walked toward her, grinning. "Looking for a book?"

Now Evie saw that his curls twisted down his forehead, almost to his brown eyes.

"Family law, right?" He paused. "Are you a student?"

Evie blushed. "No. I just like to come here and read."

"I'm not either. A student, I mean…not yet, anyway…. I'm working here for the summer. Starting classes in the fall. In law."

"You are?" she asked.

He grinned. "If you knew me better, you wouldn't be so surprised."

Evie grinned back. "Well, good luck."

"I won't need luck!" he called after her. "And my name's Nick!"

One Saturday in late summer, Nick caught up with Evie as she was leaving the library.

"Hi," he said.

"Hi."

He looked at the sky. A few puffy white clouds were floating by. "I don't like the look of those clouds," he said. "Looks like rain to me."

"Really? Those clouds?"

"You never know," he said. "I think you should get a ride home."

"Who from?" she smiled.

He held out his hand for her, as if it were the most natural thing in the world. The sensation of his palm and fingers pressing against hers sent a fire straight through her. And when he pointed to a black motorcycle leaning against the parking lot wall and grinned, she grinned back. He straddled the bike.

"Well?"

Evie squinted at him and the machine, and gathered her skirt up in one hand. With one smooth movement, she swung her leg over the seat and sat down behind him. As naturally as he'd held her hand, she slipped her arms around his waist.

He kicked the lever and the bike vibrated into life. As they sped down the streets, Evie tried to keep a respectable distance between his back and her front, but for some reason she kept sliding forward. Now she understood why people said that nice girls didn't ride motorcycles.

He stopped at her front door and put his foot on the pavement to steady the bike so she could get off, but Evie's body refused to move. Instead, her arms tightened around his waist.

"Want to keep riding?"

"Yes," she said.

Soon they were heading out of town. The old stucco shops and apartment buildings became low-slung suburban homes with spindly trees tied to stakes in their front yards. The homes gave way to farmhouses on acres of land that had not yet been sold for suburbs.

Evie had never felt that kind of freedom before. She was part of the evening air, the road, as they raced past fields, trees and farmhouses. Sometimes she rested her head against Nick's back. Sometimes she stretched away so she could feel the wind whipping her hair into her face.

Nick turned onto a rutted dirt road and Evie smelled the ocean before she saw its reflection in the sky. He stopped when the road gave way to a sandy cliff.

"I love it here," he said. "I was hoping I could show it to you someday." He let Evie slide off and then heaved the bike onto its stand. He held her hand again and led her down the path to the beach.

Children were still building sand castles as the setting sun flamed in the pink, orange and purple-streaked sky. Couples in beach chairs held hands. Nick and Evie sat against an eroding cliff.

"Tell me about yourself," she said.

"Starting when?" he laughed. "Okay, I started working in the law library about six months ago. The GI bill put me through university, but I'm going to have to pay most of my way through law school. I have a fair amount saved, but I want to have more just to be safe. Once school starts, I'm going to work part-time for a lawyer I know."

"You're a hard worker."

"It's the only way to get what I want."

"What's that?"

"To be a partner in the best law firm in San Francisco by the time I'm thirty."

"San Francisco?"

"Sierra Fortuna's a nice town, but there isn't much opportunity here."

"You're ambitious."

"Well, yeah," he said. "I grew up poor. I don't want my family to live like that."

Evie told him about the Girls' Home: the forest green trim on the glass doors of the dining room, the same color as the trestle tables inside; the clatter of cutlery; the smell of bacon fat and toast. She told him how she and her friends would skip class and sneak cigarettes from the teachers' lounge, laughing as they blew the smoke out the window. This was the version of the truth that she'd decided to remember.

Before she was finished, she realized they were leaning against each other.

"You make it sound like summer camp," he said. "Didn't you miss your parents?"

"At first, but after awhile they just didn't seem real anymore."

He shook his head. "I could never do that to my kids."

"No," she said, "I don't think I could either."

"Where are your parents now?"

"Half an hour from here." She bit her lip. "I went to see them a few months ago."

"And?"

"They were there."

He squeezed her hand.

"What about your family?" Evie asked.

He cocked his head. "My family. Well, my father was a mechanic and my mother was a nurse. There's seven of us kids. I'm the oldest. I'll take you to meet them someday."

"I'd like that." She waited a moment. "Can you tell me what you did in the war?"

"Sure. I was one of the guys who took messages between the front and the big shots way behind the lines. That's where I learned how to ride a bike. It's also where I met Albert, the lawyer I told you about. He's in real estate law now. That's going to be the next big thing, with all of us coming back and starting families and all."

For some reason, Evie blushed. She wondered what it was that made men so attractive. They looked so simple, but they held so much promise. It was more than sex. They had some elusive power that made her want to feel close to them.

He turned to her. "Where are you?"

She put her head on his shoulder. "Right here," she said.

He laced his fingers through hers and rubbed the back of her hand with his thumb. It sent shivers down her spine.

A moment later, he shifted away from her. "We should get going," he said.

They made their way back up the cliff, slipping a little on the loose sand. At the top, he held out his hand for her, and as he pulled her up, her breasts brushed against him. Evie couldn't swear she didn't do it on purpose, but she was glad they did, just to see the shock and pleasure on his face.

When they arrived back at her apartment building, he walked her up the front steps and waited while she turned the key in the lock.

"I had a wonderful time," she said. "Can we go again?"

"Whenever you like."

He waited until she went inside. She looked back just in time to see him jump up and click his feet together on the sidewalk.

Evie and Nick saw each other often that summer. Evie loved walking barefoot along the shoreline, feeling the waves bubble over her feet as they rolled in and feeling them suck the sand from under her feet as they rolled back out.

These things have always been, Evie thought. We're in this world for such a short time. We're only important to ourselves.

Sometimes they went out for dinner and a movie. Once or twice a week Evie practiced her cooking on Nick and they'd sit on the fire escape with Sassy and watch the sunset.

"Evie," Nick said on the fire escape one evening, "I can't wait any longer. I have to kiss you."

Evie tilted her head toward him. He leaned over and kissed her gently on the lips.

"Mmmm," he murmured.

She leaned over and kissed him back. This one lasted a little longer.

They kissed again. Evie felt herself melting into him. She drew away.

"I'm sorry," he said.

"No," she said. "It was nice. Too nice."

"For me, too."

But when Nick began law school, their life changed. Almost every day, he was either in class, in the law library or working for his mentor, Albert. A few days a week, he rushed to Evie's apartment for dinner before going home to study.

Occasionally they rode his bike to the beach and had a picnic. Sometimes they'd walk around one of the nicer neighborhoods in town and look at houses.

"Someday I'll buy you a house like that one," he'd say as they stopped at a dark-timbered Craftsman or a red-tile-roofed Mediterranean.

"Mmm hmm," she'd answer. She never told him she didn't care what kind of house they lived in. All she wanted was to be with him, safe and cozy in a home of their own.

In December, Nick invited Evie to a Christmas party at Albert's house. They rode between enormous wrought-iron gates and parked at the end of the driveway next to the cars, all dark, long and shiny.

Nick brushed off his pants and shrugged his jacket into place. Then he helped Evie smooth her hair. As he did, his fingers brushed her throat. They both jumped from the electricity of his touch on her skin.

Evie grabbed his hand when she saw the house. It almost looked like the Girls' Home, without the boards partly covering the windows. She felt even more unsettled when they went inside. The door opened to a large hall, which looked almost the same as the one at the Home. A curved walnut staircase led to the second floor.

But the lights were bright and the hall was filled with happy, alcohol-fueled chatter from women in sparkly gowns and men in dark, well-tailored suits.

A stocky older man rushed up to greet them. "Nick! And this must be Evie. I'm very pleased to meet you at last. I'm Al."

He and Nick shook hands and Al gave Evie a hug. "I feel as if I already know you," he said.

"Darling," he called to a woman nearby. "Come and meet Nick's exquisite Evie."

The woman took Evie's hand and pressed it between her palms. "It's lovely to meet you, my dear," she said. "Please make yourself at home. I'm sorry, but I have to see to an emergency in the kitchen."

When Evie turned back to Nick and Albert, they were talking business. She wandered off, took a glass of champagne from a waiter and leaned against the staircase's newel post.

To the left, where the dining room in the Girls' Home had been, was a large parlor. It had glass doors to close it off from the hall, like the Girls' Home had, but the trim was walnut instead of green.

Evie put her hand on the post and twisted so she could see up the stairs. She put one foot on the bottom step. She climbed each stair, her glass of champagne cold and wet in one hand, the polished railing cold and smooth in the other. The walls were a flawless creamy white. The cushiony blue carpet gave way under her feet.

There was the corridor. It had more doors than the Home had, but when she peeked in, she understood why. Every room had only one large bed and one shiny window with long, heavy drapes.

The panic came from nowhere as she reached the door that would have led to her room. Her throat began to tickle and fill with mucous. Her heart sped up and began pounding. Her chest muscles squeezed her lungs until she felt a sharp deep pain every time she forced a breath in or out.

Her champagne glass fell to the floor. Gasping, she ran down the corridor, down the stairs and out the back door, which was exactly where the back door had been at the Girls' Home. She collapsed in a dark corner of the patio, her heart racing, her lungs fighting for each ragged breath.

"Hey. Hey," she heard, and she felt an arm around her. "What's the matter?"

"I can't.... I can't...."

"Take it easy," Nick said. "Breathe with me."

As she struggled to match Nick's breaths: in and out, in and out, her chest gradually relaxed and her heartbeats slowed down. And there she slumped, exhausted, in his arms.

He brushed her sweat-drenched hair away from her face.

"What happened?" he asked again.

She took a deep, liberating breath.

"This reminds me of the Girls' Home."

She told him everything. How she ached with loneliness all those years. The bell of doom, ga dong, ga dong, ga dong. Her gorging and throwing up, her redemption, and ultimately, her freedom.

He wrapped his arms around her. "And it all came back. Oh, Evie, I'm so sorry."

"It's not your fault," she said.

"Are you angry with your parents for putting you there?"

"No," she said at last. "I know they weren't trying to hurt me. But when I got out, I didn't know what to do with the pain. I did some things that made it even worse."

"And now?" he asked.

And now?

The house glittered through the long narrow, windows. They were safe, sheltered by oak trees. Evie spoke almost before she realized how she felt.

"And now, I'm here with you."

His eyes were soft. "I will never abandon you," he said.

"But—"

"Everything that's happened to you, everything you've done, has brought you here to me," he said. "I promise you, I'll keep you safe."

He stood up and held out his hand for her. "Let's go home."

They took off down the long winding driveway and through the dark streets.

"Are you okay?" he called back to her.

"Oh, yes." Evie rested her head against his back and snuggled against him. Like heat-seeking missiles, her fingers made their way under his jacket to his shirt. She willed them to stay still, but they inched on until her palms were flat on his stomach. Then they began to knead his skin through his shirt.

"What are you doing?" he called.

"Nothing," she said. Her fingers stopped for a moment, but one of them found a gap between two buttons on his shirt. It reached through and touched his skin. Evie thought she would jump right off the seat with the thrill.

Chapter Four

Summer, 2001

The day after Nick, Evie and Kathy visit Sunset Acres, Kathy
finds her mother on the living room floor, surrounded by a
hundred years of family photographs she's pulled from albums
and scattered around herself. She's seventy-one years old, but
she can still crouch down like a teenager.

"Look," Evie says. "Here's a picture of my father. I haven't
seen it for years."

"He looks nice, Mom," Kathy says.

"Who is he again?" Evie asks.

"He's your father."

"My father?" Evie shakes her head slightly. "Oh, yes....
Can we call him?"

"He's been dead for a long time, Mom."

"How about Debby, from the Home?"

"She's dead, too,"

"And Louise?"

"I'm so sorry, Mom. She's gone, too."

Evie shakes her head. "I'm constantly looking for dead
people," she says.

Kathy stands up. "Come on," she says. "Let's go for a
walk."

Evie shuffles to the front door and shrugs on the windbreaker Kathy holds out for her. She scrabbles at the buttons.

"Here. Let me give you a hand."

Evie raises her chin like a child. There is something so wrong with this that Kathy is almost repelled. She keeps going, though, down to the very bottom one.

Kathy opens the door and watches as her mother steps onto the path. She has grown unfathomably frail this year. Kathy walks slowly, matching her steps. As they reach the end of the driveway, Brett, the neighbor down the street, stops mowing his lawn and calls out to them.

"'Morning," he says. "Beautiful day, isn't it?"

"Good morning, Brett," Evie says. "I'd like you to meet my mother, Joan."

Brett recovers first and pumps Kathy's limp hand. "We go way back, don't we?"

"You do?" Evie asks.

"Sure," Kathy says at last. "Brett taught Kevin how to box when Kevin was in high school—remember?"

"Oh, yes," Evie lies. "I remember."

"Well...." Kathy hesitates for a moment. "Brett's called us a few times. He's been worried about you."

"He has? Why?"

"Because you wander at night, Mom."

Evie's eyes turn cold. "I do no such thing," she says. "I always tell your father when I'm going out."

She stomps back to the house. Kathy shakes her head at Brett and follows her inside. Minutes later, Evie comes downstairs dragging a laundry basket full of clothing.

"I'm going home," she announces.

"Wait, Mom," Kathy begins.

At the same time, Nick says, "Evie, you are home. You live here with me."

"I do not. You're a liar!" Evie says. She drops the laundry basket, throws open the door and jerks the basket up again before either of them can move. A moment later, she's outside.

"Evie," Nick says, following her out. "Stop. You can't—"

He grabs her arm, but she has the strength to drag him to the driveway. He tries to pull her back. Clothing flies out of the basket.

"Let me go!" she cries. "Help! Help!"

Kathy watches in horror as Evie swings the basket at Nick's head. He tears it out of her hands and throws it onto the ground. Evie flails at Nick's arms, his chest. She punches, kicks and scratches. He grabs at her arms as he moves backward, but she twists away and attacks him again.

Brett runs up the street and pulls her away from Nick. "Evie! Stop it!"

She turns and claws at him.

"Call 911!" Brett yells to Kathy.

Shaking, Kathy pushes in the numbers. "We need help," she says. "My mother has Alzheimer's and she's fighting with my father on the driveway."

By the time the police arrive, Nick is sitting on the front doorstep, his head in his hands. Brett has broken away from Evie and is at the edge of the driveway, wiping blood away from his face.

Evie is picking up the clothing and throwing it back into the laundry basket. But when she spots the two officers walking toward her, she drops everything and runs through the bushes to the yard next door.

"Mom! Stop!"

Evie stops and looks back. Kathy sees the anguish in her eyes.

"Let them help you. Please, Mom."

Evie's spirit seems to leave her body. She limps as she and Kathy walk out of the bushes together. Evie is smeared with blood and twigs poke out of her sweater. Kathy leads her to the stretcher.

"Please, call Nick and tell him where they're taking me," Evie says as the paramedics help her lie down.

Kathy and Nick watch the ambulance back down the driveway.

"I can't take any more," he says. "I'm seventy-three years old. I just can't take any more."

"Do you want to go to Sunset Acres and fill out an application?"

Kathy sees the strength her father has to summon before he answers.

"Yes," he says.

Evie looks small and pale in the emergency room bed. The nurse wrapping a bandage around her leg takes one look at Nick and says, "Sit down, Sir. I'll patch you up next."

Fifteen minutes later, they're both bandaged and waiting for Dr. Fletcher.

"What did I do?" Evie asks. "What did I do?"

Nick watches in a daze as doctors and nurses discuss what happened. He hears them talking to Kathy about finding a crisis bed for Evie until Kathy and Kevin can find a permanent bed in a nursing home that takes violent patients.

Suddenly the only people in the room are Nick, Evie, Kathy and Dr. Fletcher.

Dr. Fletcher looks sternly at Nick. "This could have been much worse," he says. "Is this any way for you or Evie to live?"

"No."

"You agree to put her into a nursing home, then?"

Nick hangs his head and whispers. "Yes."

Dr. Fletcher puts his hand on Nick's shoulder. "It's the right thing to do at this point," he says. "Here's a prescription for an anti-psychotic for Evie. Give it to her instead of the sedative she's been taking."

"An anti-psychotic?" Kathy bursts out.

"It's very common in this kind of situation," the doctor says. "I've given her a very low dose. Call me if anything else comes up."

The next morning, Kathy, Nick and Evie are in the office at Sunset Acres, a sheaf of documents in front of them.

"Don't sign anything!" Evie begs. "Don't let them put me away!"

Nick's pen hangs in the air.

"Dad," Kathy says. "You have to."

"No. Don't!"

Nick looks at Evie, tears streaming down his face. "I have no choice," he says. "This isn't up to us anymore."

He signs.

"You stupid, pathetic man," she spits. "You're nothing compared to Nick."

As soon as they get back home, Evie pulls herself up the stairs and disappears into their bedroom. When Kathy looks in, she's wandering around the room, picking up the blouses, slips and nighties draped on her chair, and laying them out on the bed. Her wrists are red and swollen.

"Mom, can you come downstairs for lunch?"

"If you say so, dear."

Evie leans on Kathy on the way down. In the kitchen, the silence is so intense that the only sound is Nick's spoon scraping his soup bowl. When he pushes his chair back, Kathy and Evie both jump.

After Nick leaves the room, Evie's eyes fill with tears. "Why doesn't someone just shoot me?"

The next morning, Nick is in his easy chair, staring at the Sunset Acres documents. "What are these?" he asks Kathy.

"You signed them yesterday. Remember? You said you couldn't handle Mom's behavior anymore."

"If I signed anything, I didn't know what it was." He throws the papers into the trash.

Evie pokes her head in. "I'm going to tidy up the back bedroom," she says. "Somebody's been moving things around in there. I can't find anything."

Later that afternoon, Kathy finds Evie and Nick sitting together on the sofa.

"Dad? Mom? Can I talk to you for a minute?"

"Of course, dear." Nick almost looks happy to see her.

"Dr. Fletcher's nurse just called," Kathy says. "Dr. Fletcher wanted to know about Sunset Acre and I told him you changed your mind. He wants to see you and Mom tomorrow."

Dr. Fletcher doesn't waste any time. "Nick, I have to tell you that if you don't make a responsible decision for Evie, your children will be given the power to make it for you."

"My children will do what I tell them to."

"Then the state will take over Evie's care."

Kathy realizes that she's been holding her breath. "What if they have a caregiver?" she asks.

Nick shakes his head in disgust. "Never," he says.

"Nick," the doctor says. "I warn you, you could lose control over what happens to Evie. She could end up a hundred miles away from here."

"All right," Nick almost spits. "We'll give a caregiver a try."

The caregiver arrives a few days later. Aiden takes her to the living room where Nick is watching TV. Evie is pretending to watch.

Nick turns down the volume. "Thank you for coming," he says to the caregiver. "I'm not completely clear about why you're here, though. Can you tell me a little about what you're going to do?"

She begins confidently. "I can drive you anywhere you'd like to go, cook dinner and clean up, give Evie her evening pills and help her get ready for bed," she says. "The rest of the time, I'll just stay quietly in a corner in case you need me."

"And how much do you charge for staying quietly in a corner?" he asks.

She begins to stammer. "We…. I…."

"Dad," Kathy interrupts.

Nick stands up and holds out his right hand. "Thank you very much for coming," he says to the caregiver, "but we don't need any more help at the moment than we already have."

In the stunned silence, Kathy and the caregiver look helplessly at each other. "I'm sorry for wasting your time," Kathy says. "I'll see you out."

When Kathy gets back, she glares at Nick. "How could you do that?" she yells. "You lied to me! You said you'd let someone come in and help."

"I said no such thing."

"Yes, you did. Do you know what this means for Mom? I thought you wanted to stay together!"

Evie picks up her mug. "I'm going to the kitchen. It's too noisy in here."

"I can't even look at you," Kathy says to Nick, and storms upstairs.

It's dark when Kathy goes back downstairs. Evie is in the kitchen, moving the glasses from one cabinet to another.

"Have you seen Dad?" Kathy asks.

"No!" Evie hisses.

He's ten feet away, in the laundry room. He looks up.

"I'm sorry," Kathy says. "I don't have the right to tell you what to do."

He crosses the floor and hugs her. "We can still love each other, even if we don't agree with each other," he says.

"Even when I know best." She forces herself to smile.

He laughs. "It's late. Shouldn't you be in bed?"

Kathy falls asleep crying. She wakes up two or three times during the night. Every time, she's still crying.

1953

One Sunday in the spring, Nick picked Evie up at her apartment and took her to his home, a silvery wood-shingled farmhouse shaded by oak trees. They skidded to a stop near the end of a gravel driveway shot through with weeds and dead leaves. A big old black dog, white in the face, lumbered over to them.

"Hey, Henry," Nick said, patting him. "How're ya doin', old boy?"

Henry's hips gave out under all the affection. Nick reached down just in time to support him as he collapsed onto the ground.

"Easy, Henry, easy, boy." Nick looked up at Evie while he gently massaged Henry's hips. "He wasn't this bad the last time I was here," he said.

Evie kneeled down beside them and stroked the velvety furrow between Henry's eyes. "How old is he?"

"Almost fifteen. We got him when I was eight."

She put her arm around Nick's shoulders. "He's beautiful."

"He's been a good friend."

Evie stood up. "So," she said, "six little brothers and sisters."

Nick smiled. "Let's go see how many are home."

The front door banged open as they made their way up the path. Two little girls with hair like straw ran down the steps towards them.

"Nicky! Nicky!"

Nick bent down and caught them as they ran into him. "Hey, girls. This is my girlfriend, Evie."

They stared at her. A girl about eight years old asked, "Are you going to get married? Can I be a flower girl?"

Nick laughed. "The embarrassing one is Marilyn," he told Evie. "And this one is Betsy. Betsy, can you please take your nosy little sister and tell Mom we're here?"

Betsy grabbed at her but Marilyn wiggled away and ran to the house.

"Mommy!" she called. "Nicky's here with his girlfriend!"

Nick's mother appeared in the doorway. She had the same brown eyes and the same ruddy skin as Nick. Her curly black hair was not quite tamed in a bun just above her neck. She hugged Nick and looked a little shyly at Evie.

"I'm very pleased to meet you, my dear," she said. "Won't you come in?"

The hallway was wide and welcoming, with a thick hooked rug on the floor and delicate flowered wallpaper.

"Nick," his mother said. "Why don't you show Evie to the parlor? I'll be right there."

"You kids," they heard her call up the stairs. "Come down right now and pick up your things in the kitchen. And Sarah. Come and help make lunch."

In the parlor, Nick's mother shook her head. "Sarah was supposed to vacuum in here this morning but she went to a party last night."

"Oh, yeah? You're letting kids sleep in now?" Nick grinned.

His mother shook her head again. "It's not like when you were here. I can't keep up with them all anymore."

Nick and Evie followed her into the kitchen. Red geraniums exploded out of old coffee tins along the window ledge and on top of the battered kitchen cabinets. A green velvet sofa took up most of the far wall.

Betsy and Marilyn were sitting at a picnic table in the middle of the kitchen, holding grilled cheese sandwiches and kicking their feet. Henry the dog had lumbered in and was lying hopefully under Marilyn's seat. A teenage girl with unruly black hair turned from the stove with a frying pan in her hand.

"And this is Sarah," Nick said. "Sarah, this is Evie."

Sarah looked Evie up and down. "You look too good for him," she grinned.

Their mother smiled. "You just make sure you don't burn those sandwiches," she said.

Nick ran his hand along the table. "I remember when Dad and I built this, after Meggie was born," Nick said.

"We outgrew the old one," his mother said. "It seemed that we had a new baby almost every year back then."

"I can't imagine having so many children," Evie said.

"We lost two after Annie was born. We would have had nine."

She looked away for a moment, and then she sat beside Evie. "Tell me a little about yourself, my dear."

Evie kept it short. She'd moved from Mariposa to become a receptionist in a law office in Santa Fortuna. She'd been a legal secretary for almost a year, and had met Nick in the university's law library.

"The law library?" his mother asked. "Is that part of your job?"

Evie blushed. "No."

His mother was still looking at her.

"I thought, maybe someday, I'd go to university and I might try to get into law school."

"What?" Nick said.

"I've never told anyone before."

"Well, I'm glad you told us," his mother said. "You seem smart enough to be a lawyer. Don't you think, Nick?"

"Oh, yeah, sure. But a woman lawyer?"

"It's just something I was thinking about," Evie said, wishing she hadn't mentioned it.

Nick's mother patted her hand. "I think you're a very wise woman to be making plans for your future."

When they finished lunch, Nick took Evie for a walk in the field behind the house. The air smelled of warm, fertile soil. The grasses and wildflowers hummed with the sounds of insects feeding on nectar.

Evie slipped her hand into Nick's. "Some of you kids are so fair-skinned," she said, "and your mother and you and Sarah look almost…."

He let go of her hand.

"Colored? That's because we are. Or were. Or are. I don't know. My mother's grandmother or great-grandmother came here from the South in the old slave days. She was a maid in this house and looked after the children. Their mother died, and a few years later, my great-grandfather, or whoever he was, married her and they had more children. Scandalous, but generations of kids grew up here and somehow my mother inherited the house. She's been hanging onto it ever since."

"You're lucky to know something about your past. Neither of my parents ever wanted to talk about their families."

Nick held her hand again. They passed a rusted, half-buried wheelbarrow overflowing with purple sage and bright orange

California poppies. Clusters of delicate bell-shaped flowers hung from manzanita trees and bright red berries hung from toyons. The oaks rose above them all, their branches sheltering the bare soil around them. And in the distance, the velvety green mountains.

They wandered to a grove of sycamores and sat in the shade.

"It must have been wonderful growing up here," Evie said.

"I know it seems that way." Nick pulled up a blade of grass from a clump of fescue and began peeling it into even narrower strips.

"My father died out here," he said.

"What?"

"You might as well know. He tried to drink himself to death, but I guess that was taking too long because he blew his brains out."

"No!"

"Over there."

Nick gestured beyond the sycamores to the remains of a dozen cars. Some were completely rusted out. Some lurched at odd angles, with tires, doors and anything else that was removable missing.

"When Marilyn was still a baby. My brother Patrick found him in one of the cars. After the ambulance took Dad away, Patrick and I drove the car into the lake over the hill there."

"Nick. No."

"He had a bad back from an injury in World War I, so he had a small disability pension. He did okay working part-time as a mechanic, but after he lost his job, he spent most of his days out here, drinking. When he died, Mom got a good pension as his widow, so she quit working at the hospital to look after the younger kids. They're actually better off now than when he was alive. But I know Mom feels the weight of it every day. So do I. I feel like we're all tainted."

He looked at her with hopeless eyes. "Now you know."

"I'm glad you told me."

"So?" he asked, as if he didn't want to know the answer. "What do you think?"

"I think everybody has something," Evie said, in an echo of her father. "We can't know what anyone else's pain feels like. Your father probably didn't see any way out. It doesn't mean you're like him, or you inherited it from him, if that's what you're worried about. But I think that's what's going to make you the man you're going to become."

He looked at her, his eyes soft. "That's what I think, too."

He broke off another blade of grass and began peeling it.

"The thing is, even when he was drinking he was a great father. He made us dinner when Mom was working. When his back wasn't bothering him too much, he taught us how to fish and play ball and fix cars, even the girls. He used to let the little kids fall asleep watching TV and I'd carry them up to bed. I know he loved us."

His voice broke.

"Do you wonder how he could have left you?" Evie asked.

"All the time. Why weren't we enough for him to keep going?"

"I wonder the same thing. What was wrong with me that my parents didn't take me back from the Home?"

"Will you lie down with me?" he asked. "I want to hold you."

They held each other in the sweet-smelling grass, hip to hip, belly to belly, heart to heart.

"I'm glad you came with me today," Nick said once they were back in Evie's apartment. "I wanted to tell you about my father before, but...."

Something in his voice had changed. There was a gentleness, an intimacy, that hadn't been there before. It was in his eyes and in his touch as he caressed her hair and let it slide between his fingers.

Evie closed her eyes and nestled against his chest. "I love you," she said, before she had time to think.

"I love you, too." His voice was thick. "And I want to marry you. Evelyn Madison, will you marry me?"

"Oh, yes."

It was late summer before Nick had time to go with Evie to see her parents. Evie's father was standing on the front porch, shielding his eyes from the sun and scanning the road. He limped toward the driveway as they turned in.

"Welcome! Welcome!" he said as Nick stopped the motorcycle. "It's wonderful to see you, my dear. You too, young fellow." He put his hand on Nick's shoulder.

"I'm pleased to meet you, Sir," Nick said.

Evie gave her father a little hug. "Hi Daddy."

"Come on into the living room," her father said. "Mother insisted on getting out of bed to see you."

"Your father really loves you," Nick whispered as he and Evie followed him in. "You should've seen his face when you hugged him."

Evie's mother looked tiny, bent over in her wheelchair in the darkened room. "Who is this?" she asked. "Is it Evie and her young man?"

Evie crouched beside the wheelchair. "Yes, Mom, I'm here, and I've brought Nick with me."

"Let me see him."

Nick crouched down beside her. "I'm right here, Mrs. Madison. I'm very pleased to meet you."

Evie's mother put her hand on Nick's. Her eyes were red-rimmed. "You look like a kind young man," she said.

"Thank you, Ma'am."

"Sit down, my boy," Evie's father said.

Evie had moved back toward the front hall. The weight of her parents' happiness was too much to bear. Still, when Nick motioned for her to sit down beside him, she did.

He held Evie's hand. "Mr. and Mrs. Madison," he said, "one of the reasons I'm happy to be here is that I want to ask your permission to marry your daughter."

"Will you take care of her?" her father asked.

"Till the day I die."

"Do you love him?" her mother asked Evie.

"Yes, Mom," Evie said. "I do."

Her father stood up and shook Nick's hand. "Well, then, you have our blessing," he said.

"Thank you, Sir. I'll make her happy, I promise."

There was a long, deep silence. Nick suddenly realized that Evie was trembling. He put his arm around her.

"Why did you leave me there?" she whispered. "Was I really so bad?"

"Oh, Evie. You weren't bad," her father said. "You weren't bad at all. You were such a lovely little girl. We never dreamed you'd be there for so long. All of a sudden, you were eighteen."

"Well, it wasn't sudden for me," she said. The harshness of her voice surprised even her. "You never came to visit me. Not once. You never even wrote me a letter in all those years. Did you think about me at all?"

Her parents looked like she'd hit them.

"Evie," Nick said.

"Why did I have to pay?" she cried. "Why didn't they?"

"Evie. Please."

Nick felt her straighten. She clung to his hand. "You're right. I'm sorry."

But it was too late.

"I'd like to go back to bed now," Evie's mother said.

"Of course, Mother." Her father's voice caught on the name. "You don't mind seeing yourselves out, do you?"

Inside Evie's apartment, Nick held her and smoothed her hair. "You know, Evie, you aren't the only one who's hurt."

"But they left me. I didn't leave them."

"I don't understand why your mother felt that she couldn't look after you. But she put you in a place where she knew you'd be safe. Doesn't that count for something?"

"But after my father came home...."

He sighed. "Your father came home with one arm and a bum leg. Who knows what he went through?"

"Lucky he didn't have me around to make things harder."

"You can feel sorry for yourself if you want," he said. "But is that the way you want to live? Wouldn't you rather spend it being happy with me?"

Evie was silent.

He got up and walked to the door. "Let me know what you decide."

Evie didn't hear from him the next day.

"You can always call him, you know," Sheila told her.

"No, thanks," Evie said. "He left. He can call me if he wants to."

The next morning, a deliveryman brought a bouquet of red roses to Evie's desk at work. Nick had written the card himself: "I'd like to talk to you."

"You have to call him," Sheila said. "If you love him, you have to listen to what he has to say."

On her lunch break, Evie walked to the university and found Nick's bike. She clipped the stem of one of the roses onto the carrier at the back.

She was washing the dishes that evening when her doorbell rang. Nick walked in.

"Come over here," he said. He led her to the sofa and held her hands. "I've been thinking. I love you. But the other day, I wasn't sure you loved me."

Evie opened her mouth.

"Let me finish. No matter how much we love each other, there will always be times when one of us isn't sure that the other one loves us back. Can we both trust that we love each other, even when we're most afraid that the other one doesn't?"

That was a leap Evie hadn't considered before.

"Well?"

"I don't know," she said. "Maybe. I'll try."

"So will I."

He leaned in to her and kissed her. Her blood shimmered in her veins. She loved his smell, his skin, the hairs on his arms. They fell onto the sofa and made love with such intensity that Evie had no idea where her body ended and where his began.

1954

In February, Evie and Nick rode to see Sheila and Edgar in their apartment. It had been full of promise when they'd moved in a little more than two years before, newly painted and carpeted and stocked with wedding presents.

The last time Evie had been there, it had looked cozy and domestic, with cushions tossed on the sofa and a crib against one wall. Sheila had been wrapped in a quilt in the rocking chair, feeding Sophie a bottle of milk, and Edgar had been putting the vacuum cleaner away.

This time when Edgar opened the door, a whiff of cloth diapers that had gone too long without washing wafted into the hallway. Toys and newspapers littered the living room floor. A twin mattress leaned against the crib.

"Sorry the place is such a mess," Edgar said, scooping up Sophie as she began toddling out the door. "I've been busy at work and Sheila—"

"Sheila what?" came Sheila's voice from the kitchen. "I can hear you, you know."

"I was about to say that Sheila, my beautiful wife, is great with child again and unable to bend down and pick anything up off the floor," Edgar called back.

"Any excuse, right?" Evie said as she picked her way across the living room to the kitchen. She took one look at Sheila in an old plaid shirt of Edgar's over a maternity dress, stirring a pot on the stove and cried, "Oh my god, Sheila, you're huge!"

"Thanks. I didn't realize that," Sheila said. "Yesterday I tried to jump up and sit on the counter and my boobs hit me in the face. Believe me, I'm never doing this again."

"You're going to stop having sex with Edgar?" Evie hissed.

"Of course not," Sheila said. "It's too much fun. At least that's the way I remember it. I'm going to have a hysterectomy."

"Isn't that a little drastic?"

"It's the only way to be sure I don't get pregnant again. I feel like a baby machine. I just have to find a way to talk my doctor into letting me have it."

She put her hand on her back and stretched. "Evie, do you mind stirring for me for awhile?"

She groaned as she sank into a chair at the kitchen table.

"Are you okay?" Evie asked.

Sheila smiled wanly, but her eyes were as bright as always. "Yes," she said. "I am. I know this doesn't look like much, but we're happy, Evie. I wouldn't have it any other way."

In the living room, Edgar looked at Nick and shook his head. "I love Sheila and Sophie, but I don't know what we're going to do. Sophie's going to have to sleep on the mattress on the floor after the baby's born. I just don't earn enough to be able to move to a bigger place."

"You're a good salesman," Nick said. "Have you thought of going into real estate? It's going to be huge."

A light flashed in Edgar's tired eyes. "No," he said. "I hadn't."

"I can talk to a couple of people if you like."

As soon as he had a chance, Nick pulled Evie into the bedroom. "I don't think we should get married for awhile," he said.

"What?"

He held her hands in his. "Evie, I love you and I do want to marry you, but I couldn't live like this. I want to be able to take care of you. Properly. I can't do that until I have a job.'"

"I don't need you to take care of me, Nick. All I need is for you to love me."

"I do love you," he said. "But–"

He saw a wall clang down in front of her eyes.

"All right," she said. "Fine. Whatever you want."

"Evie. What?"

"I want to go home."

She marched to the kitchen to say goodbye, but she faltered at the doorway. Edgar was holding the baby and leaning over Sheila as she stirred the pot. The three of them looked so in love with each other, her heart shattered.

"You will never, ever be surrounded by love like that," a voice within her said. "Count yourself lucky that you have a cat."

Evie didn't have any trouble keeping plenty of space between herself and Nick on the ride home. When they arrived at her apartment, she slipped off the back of his bike and started up the steps.

"Don't bother coming in," she said.

"Evie. I think we should talk."

"About what?" She slammed the front door behind her.

She had barely locked her apartment door when Nick knocked.

"Evie. Please let me in."

She opened the door. Nick walked in and sat on the sofa.

"I'm not going to apologize," he said. "You know how I grew up. Our parents loved us, and each other, but they didn't have enough money and that affected...everything. Seeing Sheila and Edgar brought it all back to me. I don't want that for my family."

Evie knew what he wasn't saying. That he was terrified that he'd end up like his father.

"Are you willing to wait?" he asked again.

"I'm willing to wait."

He let out a sigh. "Good. Because it would take me a long time to find someone else I'd love as much as I love you."

Sassy jumped onto the sofa. She was still a stray at heart, but now she sprawled on her back across both their laps and purred like a buzz saw. Evie felt exactly the same way as Edgar, Sheila and Sophie had looked to her.

One hot July morning, Evie woke up feeling Nick behind her, caressing her ribs, down the valley of her waist, over the hill of her hips, and back again. She turned and they made love again, slowly, languidly, their bodies already in tune.

Afterward, she said, "Let's go to the beach today."

Nick rolled over. "I can't. I have to work on an assignment."

"But it's Sunday. And we just...."

He exhaled and nodded. "Yes, we did. But I have to, Evie."

She put her hand on his leg. "But once you're a lawyer, you won't be so busy, right?"

He was silent for a moment. That would have told her something if she'd been paying attention, but he was stroking her again.

"Why don't you come over to my place tonight? I'll cook dinner to make it up to you."

She was reaching for him when the phone rang.

"I'm sorry for calling so early." Evie could barely hear her father's voice. "But I have some bad news. Your mother died in her sleep last night."

She passed the phone to Nick.

"It's my father. I don't understand what he said."

"Hello, Sir. This is Nick."

A moment's silence.

"Mm hum. I'm very sorry to hear that, Sir. I'll tell Evie."

He hung up. "I'm sorry, Evie."

In his arms, blind, Evie saw her mother's face. Full of joy when she'd picked Evie up at the Girls' Home; devastated, Evie now realized, when Evie told her she was moving out; and happy, so pitifully happy, to see her with Nick.

Evie had believed that any love that might have connected her and her mother had been replaced by pain that kept them apart. But, she wondered, was it possible to feel pain without love? Had she been wrong all along?

Evie took the bus to her parents' house the next day. Nick planned to ride down the day after that for the funeral.

The once white walls of the house had become dingy with time. Dried palm fronds hung from the red tile roof and the yellow, orange and blue bird of paradise flowers had died, leaving only their shredded beige beaks and crests. The manicured green lawn looked as if it was in front of the wrong house.

Her father opened the door while she was still climbing the steps. He was leaning heavily on his cane. His stomach looked almost concave. When he held her, she felt him trembling.

"Thank you for coming, my dear," he said.

They stood awkwardly on the porch. "Come in, come in," he said at last. "I'll get you some iced tea."

Evie followed him into the kitchen. "I'm sorry for what I said the last time I was here," she said.

"Oh, honey. You never have to apologize to me."

"And I'm sorry about Mom. I know I wasn't...."

He sat on one of the kitchen chairs and wiped his eyes with his sleeve. "Your mother was so proud of you," he said. "And she was happy that you were making a good life for yourself. That's all you need to think about."

"Are you...?"

"I'm fine."

But he faltered.

"I miss her, more than anything." He burst into an explosion of sobs. "I don't know what I'm going to do without her."

"Oh, Daddy." Evie bent down and hugged him.

"I'm sorry," he said. He pushed back his chair and stumbled upstairs.

Evie cleaned out as much of the dirt, sadness and decay as she could. She went through the rooms downstairs and opened all the curtains and windows. She threw out the old newspapers and carried the dirty dishes into the kitchen. She washed the dishes, vacuumed the carpets, got down on her hands and knees and scrubbed the kitchen floor.

The phone and the doorbell rang all afternoon. People brought meals, offered to help, sent flowers. It was overwhelming, really. Evie had never considered that her parents had a life outside their home.

She heated one of the casseroles for dinner. Her father sat with the plate in front of him, but he didn't pick up his fork.

"Maybe later," he said, and shuffled back to their room. His room, now.

The next morning, Nick rode up on his bike. Evie melted into his hug.

"How're you doing?" he asked.

"I'm fine. My father's hardly come downstairs, though."

"I'll go and see him."

Half an hour later, Nick and her father came down the stairs together. Her father had his hand on Nick's shoulder.

"You've chosen a fine young man," he said.

They piled into the car, with Nick in the driver's seat.

"I didn't know you could drive a car," Evie teased.

"I have all kinds of talents you still don't know about yet." Nick grinned into the rear view mirror.

They turned off the highway onto a narrow paved road that curved through scrub oaks and eucalyptus trees. A white clapboard church with a narrow steeple came into view, and then a parking lot that was almost filled with cars. Clumps of people, all of them wearing black, were making their way into the church.

Evie and Nick walked beside her father through the parking lot, up the concrete steps and inside the church with its golden oak pews and its vaulted ceiling, pure white and trimmed in garlands of blue and gold. They paused every few seconds as people spoke to her father. He didn't seem to hear. He sank heavily onto the pew. He didn't look up once during the entire service.

Evie lost track of the minister's words. Surrounded by the beauty of the church and by the strangers who'd come together for only one reason, because they cared about her parents, she was lulled into a feeling of belonging that she hadn't felt since she'd left the Girls' Home. That feeling had come with anger and pain, though. Evie yearned for this peaceful acceptance and love.

After her mother's coffin had been lowered into the deep earthen rectangle in the grass, Evie, Nick and Evie's father walked back to the church's social room, where the women had placed sandwiches, jelled salads, sliced meats and as many pies, cakes and cookies as Evie had seen in most bakeries.

She was picking up a triangle of an egg salad sandwich when a sturdy woman in a shiny black dress and hat bustled over to her. The woman placed her hand on Evie's arm.

"My dear, I'm so glad you came," she said.

"Of course—" Evie began.

"I'm Elizabeth Stockton," the woman continued. "I'm an old friend of your parents."

"Oh—"

"Your father is such a good man. He was wonderful with your mother right to the end."

"I'm—"

"I was hoping to see you here, my dear. I've been wanting to talk to you." The woman edged Evie over to a bench. She gestured for her to sit down and sat beside her.

"I became a very good friend of your mother when your parents first moved here." Mrs. Stockton paused, but only for a moment. "It seemed that all the other couples our age were having babies left and right. My husband—God rest his soul—and I had four without even trying. But your parents...."

She shrugged and shook her head. "When they found out they were going to have you, they were thrilled. But when you were born...your mother didn't know what to do with you. Her own mother had died of the typhoid when your mother was a baby, so she didn't get very much mothering herself. My husband and I felt so sad for you."

Evie resented this busybody in the shiny black dress, but more than that, she hated that the woman could make her cry. "Why are you telling me this?" she almost shouted. "I don't want to hear it."

"I think you need to hear it, my dear. You didn't have the life a child deserves, but I wanted you to know that your parents loved you dearly and they did the best they could."

The woman patted her arm. "I hope you've found it in your heart to forgive them," she said. "For your own happiness if nothing else."

Nick walked Evie up to her apartment when they got back from the funeral. "Do you want me to stay?" he asked.

"I just want to take a bath and go to sleep. Do you mind?"

He kissed her. "I'll call you in the morning."

Evie lay in bed curled around Sassy, kneading her warm fur. A long-buried memory of her mother stroking her, comforting her, pierced her so suddenly that she caught her breath with the pain.

And then in the blackness, the void, and the pain filling the void, filling her.

"Mommy!"

Sassy jumped off the bed and Evie was alone on the top bunk.

Not the top bunk. She was in her own bed, in her own apartment. She had a soft orange cat that licked her with her sandpaper tongue. She had a man who loved her. She was loved. She was loved.

Chapter Five

The morning after Nick sends the caregiver away, Kathy calls Kevin.

"Do you think his not wanting a caregiver has anything to do with money?" Kathy asks.

"No," Kevin says. "They've always been careful with their money. I think he could afford it if he wanted to."

"Then why not, when the alternative is so much worse? Do you think he doesn't want to be responsible for making the decision?"

"I think he's grasping on to some sense of control over his life." Kevin says. "He's already been told he can't drive and now he's being told he can't take care of Mom. It's just too much for him to lose."

"What can we do, then?"

"I don't think we should do anything."

"What?"

"Dr. Fletcher is doing his job, but his job is to try to keep them safe. I think our job is to try to balance their safety with Dad's self-respect and their love for each other. And I think that trumps her disease."

"But what if Dad gets sick? What would happen to her then?"

"If they stay at home without any more care than they have now, what's the worst that could happen?" he counters.

"They could die."

"But is that really the worst?" he persists. "Worse than separating them after forty-six years? Worse than what's ahead for her? You know she always told us that she'd rather die than end up like this."

"She told me she probably wouldn't be here next year," Kathy says. "When I asked her where she'd be, she pointed to the ground and said she wouldn't mind. It's amazing, this duty to live life to the end, even when she says she's had enough."

"Maybe she hasn't really had enough, though. When she recognizes Dad and they're together, they're so loving and tender, I envy them. That might be enough to keep her going even when she doesn't remember him. And enough for him."

"The worst thing would be for them to suffer," Kathy says.

"Don't you think forcing them apart would make them suffer more than anything else?"

There's a very short silence.

"Yes, I do," she says. "I don't think we have the right to pressure him to make this decision, at least not yet. He really does love her. He still calls her his bride."

"And she loves him, when she isn't trying to kill him," he says.

Two weeks later, Kevin's cell phone rings just before he arrives at his pet clinic. "Uncle Kevin, Grandma and Grandpa's neighbor just called me. The paramedics are taking Grandpa to emergency," Aiden says. "He's having chest pains. I'm going to the house and stay with Grandma. She's going crazy. She thinks he's been arrested."

Kevin turns around, stops off at his house to pack a bag and drives straight to Nick and Evie's. Aiden meets him at the door and barrels into his arms.

"Oh, Uncle Kevin. I'm so glad you're here. We're supposed to go and see Grandpa at the hospital and Grandma won't come downstairs. I don't know what to do."

"You're a trooper." Kevin gives her a squeeze. "I'm going to stay here for a few days, so you can go if you like."

Aiden flies out the door.

Kevin is making ham and eggs for lunch when Evie comes downstairs. She's wearing two dressing gowns. She looks at the frying pan in dismay.

"Oh, Kevin, you didn't have to do that," she says.

"I wanted to," he says cheerfully. Too cheerfully.

"Well, it's wonderful to see you. Dad will be down in a minute."

"He's still in the hospital," Kevin says. "Do you remember the ambulance came this morning?"

"Oh, yes. I forgot. I think they said he could come home later today."

They drive to the hospital after Evie's nap. Nick is asleep. Evie sits in a chair beside him, leaning toward him, perfectly still. They both look very fragile.

"They say it was a heart attack," Nick brags when he wakes up. "I can't even walk to the bathroom."

Kevin and Evie spend most of the next two weeks driving to and from the hospital, every morning and afternoon. The morning they arrive at his room to pick him up, Dr. Fletcher is there.

Dr. Fletcher motions Kevin into the hall. "Your father isn't going to recover fully from this heart attack," he says, "and he won't survive the next one. You and your sister have to take control of this situation right now."

"We've asked him to put Mom in a nursing home, but he refuses."

"Then you'll have to get power of attorney for her health care and do it yourselves."

"He'll never give to us power of attorney."

"Then you have to take it. You go to court, with your father there, and tell the judge why you believe he isn't competent to make decisions on your mother's behalf."

"You aren't serious," Kevin says.

"When it's in the best interest of the parent, it's the only thing to do. Contact the Office of the Public Guardian. And try doubling up on the anti-psychotic for your mother and see if it makes any difference."

Once the doctor is far enough down the corridor, Kevin calls Kathy.

"Can you imagine having to face him in court?" Kevin says. "How could we possibly do that to him?"

"We don't have to actually do it," she says. "We could just tell him we could do it."

"You tell him," Kevin says. "He always liked you best."

At the curb, Nick moves gingerly from the wheelchair to the front seat of the car.

"I'm as good as ever," he claims. Once he makes it upstairs, though, he sleeps for the rest of the day. Evie spends most of the day lying beside him.

When Kevin goes downstairs the next morning, she's eating crackers out of the box.

"Is that what you're having for breakfast?" he asks.

"This is what I always have," Evie says.

"You have to eat properly if you and Dad want to stay in the house together."

"We're eating perfectly well," she says. "Meals on Wheels comes twice a week. We order those delicious salads from the pizza place. Aiden cooks dinner. I cook," she lies.

"Aiden says all you eat is canned soup when she isn't here, and that the freezer in the garage is full of food from Meals on Wheels."

"Soup is very nourishing," Evie says.

Nick arrives in time to hear the last of the conversation. "We're doing just fine, thank you."

Suddenly, Kevin is exhausted. All he can see for the future is more frantic trips to rescue his parents, more pressure on his wife, Chela, working without him at their pet clinic, and more time away from his family.

"You aren't doing fine," Kevin tells him. "You just had a heart attack because of the stress you're under."

"That isn't true," Nick says.

"And I had to drop everything to come here and look after Mom while you were in the hospital. What if I couldn't have?"

"Look after me?" Evie says. "I can take perfectly good care of myself. You're crazy."

"That will be the day, when we can't take care of ourselves." Nick pushes his chair back. "I'll be in my office."

The force of their outrage quickens Kevin's heart. His palms are sweating, he realizes. In the long, long silence, he chooses to fight, for their lives. He pushes himself away from the table and heads upstairs.

Nick is hunched forward in his chair, staring at the computer screen.

"Dad," Kevin says. "There's something else I have to tell you."

He waits for a moment and pulls the trigger for the last time.

"Dr. Fletcher wants Kathy and me to challenge your power of attorney for Mom and put her into a nursing home without your consent. We'll do it, I swear, for both your sakes. You've done an amazing job looking after her all this time but you just cannot keep this up. No one could, without more help than you have now. You know the stress landed you in the hospital. What would happen if you didn't make it out the next time?"

Nick looks startled for a moment, as if he hadn't considered that he might be mortal. "Well, then she'd go into a nursing home," he says. "But not while I'm still alive."

The evening after Kevin's ultimatum to Nick, Evie and Nick lie side by side in bed. This is the same place they made their children, looked after each other when they were sick, worked out their problems with their children, their work, each other. The backs of their hands touch, so familiar, as if they're part of the same body.

"The noose is tightening," she says.

"They'll never leave us alone," he says. "We have to get away from here."

"But how? They won't let you drive."

He squeezes her hand. "But the car is still in the garage."

"Nick!" He can hear the admiration in her voice. "But where can we go?"

"Vancouver, We could stay with Edgar and Sheila."

"And Debby," she says. "Is Debby still alive?"

"No. She died a few years ago."

"Oh, yes," she says absently.

"I'd love to see Sheila again," she says. "It'll be just like the old days, before everyone started interfering in our lives."

He nuzzles her hair. "What do they know? We can do just fine on our own."

"We'll show them."

"Let's leave as soon as Kevin goes home."

1954

The morning after Evie's mother's funeral, the phone woke Evie up.

"Why don't you take the day off work today," Nick said. "We can go to the beach. I'll bring lunch."

Evie was standing on the steps of her apartment as he rode up.

"Jump on!"

They carried the cooler down the cliff and unpacked it on an old quilt. At the bottom of the cooler was a tiny blue box.

He picked it up. "I brought this, too," he said, looking happy and embarrassed at the same time. "My mother gave it to me when we were there. Do you want to open it?"

Inside was the most beautiful diamond ring Evie had ever seen. Eight small round stones surrounded a larger one: a daisy made of diamonds.

"Oh Nick. It's beautiful."

"It was her mother's. Here, put it on."

It stopped at her knuckle.

"We can take it to a jeweler and have it made bigger," he said. "If you still want to marry me."

"Yes," she said. "I still want to marry you."

Nick passed his bar exam in August, a few weeks after Evie's mother died. Instead of joining the largest law firm in San Francisco, he went to work for his mentor, Albert.

"There's plenty of opportunity in Sierra Fortuna," he told Evie, "and we're thinking about opening an office in San Francisco."

They had a small wedding in October. Sheila and Edgar were the matron of honor and the best man. Nick's sister, Marilyn, finally got her wish and was a flower girl.

At the reception, Albert's wife took Evie aside. "I hope you know what you're getting into, my dear. Nick is just like Al. He'll love you with all his heart, but he'll live for his work."

"Thank you," Evie said, "but he promised me that once he became a lawyer he'd be able to spend more time with me."

Albert's wife put her hand on Evie's arm. "Yes, well, I wish you both the best, my dear."

Nick and Evie left all the boxes that Nick had brought from his old apartment scattered on her living room floor and rode to a cabin up the coast for their honeymoon. They had more fun, in and out of bed, than Evie could have imagined. Her only disappointment was that they had to leave a day early because Nick had to help Albert with a last minute change in one of his cases.

Nick had been right about real estate becoming the next big thing. By 1954 the baby boom was in full swing and so was the demand for homes. When he did come home in time for dinner, he always brought a briefcase full of documents to work on, usually late into the evening.

About a year after they were married, Evie found out she was pregnant. Nick was thrilled. She wasn't sure how she felt.

They bought a two-story Mediterranean-style house in the nicest new suburb in Sierra Fortuna. The white stucco walls shone in the sunlight. The lawn was bright green, but the spindly trees and shrubs in the front yard were barely visible.

Evie decorated the house herself. She still held out hope that her marriage was going to turn out the way she'd expected. Nick loved her, she was certain of that.

"I hope I'll be able to be home more once the baby's born," he said, "but until then, I really have to keep this up."

1956

Kathy was born in June. Evie fell in love with her the instant the nurse put her in her arms. So did Nick, and Sassy, who watched over her like a guard dog.

Evie had assumed that as long as Kathy was fed and rested and dry, she'd be gurgling with happiness while she was awake. Instead, nothing seemed to stop her from crying, day and night. The tiny red-faced baby began to torture Evie, always seeming to need something that Evie had no idea how to give.

For weeks, Evie followed the doctor's advice to get Kathy on a four-hour feeding schedule so she wouldn't become spoiled. But by the time Evie got her bottle to exactly the right temperature, Kathy was usually screaming too hysterically to eat or asleep from exhaustion.

She squirmed so much when Evie put on her diapers that Evie never managed to pin them so they didn't leak. And if by some miracle she did get Kathy to fall asleep in her lap, she'd spend hours trapped in the rocking chair with her arm numb, afraid to move a muscle in case Kathy woke up.

Nick, who had fed, changed and rocked to sleep almost all his brothers and sisters, was no help. "Really, Evie," he said one evening, "don't you have any maternal instinct at all?"

The next day, she drove to see Sheila in the new bungalow she and Edgar had bought since he'd gone into real estate.

"I don't know what to do," Evie cried. "I can't look after my own baby."

Sheila took the squalling Kathy from her. "Of course you can. You just have to relax. She's probably a little colicky, that's all."

And with Kathy nestled quietly into her shoulder, Sheila filled a bowl with hot water and set her bottle inside to warm up. A few minutes later, she tapped a few drops of the formula onto her wrist.

"Here," Sheila commanded. "Sit down."

Sheila put a protesting Kathy onto Evie's lap. She positioned the baby so Kathy could drink comfortably and gave Evie the bottle. "Just relax, Evie. Trust yourself. There, you'll get it."

When Nick arrived home that evening, Evie was holding a sleeping Kathy in the rocking chair. He kissed them both.

"It looks like you're getting the hang of it," he said.

"I took her to Sheila's today," Evie said. "She helped. But I wish you could spend more time with us. You're so good with her."

"You know I have to keep up with work, especially now," he said. "I'm glad to see you holding her. She needs to feel close to you."

"But I need to feel close to you."

He sighed. "This case will be over in a few weeks. Why don't the three of us go back up the coast for a couple of days after that?"

Evie weighed the reality of the present against the promise of the future. "Okay," she said reluctantly.

Kathy was almost six months old before Nick could take a weekend off from work. The morning before their trip, Evie fed her and put her to bed for her nap. She spent the rest of the morning dumping dirty clothes and diapers into her new wringer washer, feeding them between the rollers to squeeze the water out and hanging them on the clothesline in the back yard to dry.

In the afternoon, she fed Kathy and put her in her playpen, dragged two suitcases from the garage up to the bedroom and heaved them onto the bed. She went back outside and brought in the sun-scented laundry, folded it and put it away.

Kathy woke up screaming. She lashed out with her arms and legs when Evie picked her up and screamed for almost half an hour, her face wet and red and her body rigid. Evie walked her around the living room with tears of exhaustion rolling down her face.

That was when Nick came home.

"What's the matter with her? Here, give her to me." He grabbed Kathy from Evie. Evie watched as her sobs faded and she fell asleep on Nick's shoulder.

His lip curled. "Why can't you do this?" he asked.

Evie backed away.

"Something came up at work and I can't get away this weekend, so don't go to any trouble," he said.

"What?"

"I'm sorry, but it's important."

"So is going away this weekend. For me. Why isn't that as important as work you do every day?" she asked.

"We've been through this before, Evie. There's nothing else I can say."

Nick carried Kathy to her room.

Evie and Nick settled into a life of mild discontentment. When Nick was in town, he spent his days and evenings working. Evie spent her days with Kathy and her evenings alone.

Most mornings she'd put Kathy in her stroller and take her up the hill to the playground. Kathy would toddle over to some children with a smile and her bouncing brown curls and soon she'd be laughing and running along with them.

Evie, on the other hand, could never think of anything to say to the other mothers about toilet training or feeding picky eaters. She watched in awe as they swooped in and pulled children away from flying wooden swings. They always remembered to bring snacks.

"All you have to do is what the other mothers are doing," Nick told her. "How hard can that be?"

Most days Evie and Nick hardly talked at all. If he wasn't in San Francisco trying to drum up clients for the new office, he usually arrived home after Kathy was in bed and worked in the den until Evie was asleep.

"Sometimes I think you'd rather work than have sex with me," Evie complained one evening.

"We had sex three days ago." He didn't even look up from his desk.

"A week and a half," she said. "I wrote it on the calendar."

"You did what? Oh, never mind. Maybe if you were awake when I got to bed, we'd have sex more often."

"Maybe if you got to bed before midnight, I'd be awake."

He glared at her. "What, do you write that on the calendar, too?"

Nick left for work the next day, a Sunday, before Evie woke up. After breakfast, she walked Kathy to Sheila and Edgar's new house a few blocks away. It had taken only a year for them to trade up to a rambling two-story Craftsman, their dream home.

Sheila had morphed into the wife of a successful businessman as easily as she used to turn the pages of her fashion magazines. This morning, her hair was perfectly set, teased and sprayed in the same style as Jackie Kennedy, the sophisticated wife of a popular senator back East.

Evie's hair fell straight almost to her shoulders. And instead of a pretty sun dress like Sheila's, Evie wore a bright cotton blouse and long summer pants.

In the back yard, Kathy scrambled out of her stroller and ran stiff-legged to Edgar, who was pushing their two daughters on the swing set. Edgar swung Kathy into the air. The two girls jumped off their swings and hugged her until they all collapsed into a laughing pile on the grass.

"Evie, it's great to see you." Edgar bent down and kissed her cheek. "How's Nick?"

Evie's eyes filled with tears. "We just had another fight."

Edgar looked at Sheila.

"Go on," she said.

Evie saw him sigh with relief. He put his hand on her shoulder. "I hope you both can work it out," he said, and went back to play with the girls.

Sheila poured Evie a glass of iced tea.

"I don't know what to do," Evie said. "I get angry because he'd rather be working than be with us, and then I start a fight and that makes everything even worse."

"Are you at least having sex?" Sheila asked. "If you lose that, you'll lose everything."

"I guess I've lost everything, then."

Sheila sat back in her chair and sighed. "This reminds me of when we first met and I had to teach you how to dress and put on makeup. Do I still have to tell you how to do everything?"

Evie smiled, for the first time in a very long time. "Apparently," she said.

"Wait here." Sheila went inside and came back out with a stack of magazines and paperbacks six inches high. "Take these home," she said. "Read the magazines any time, but read the books in bed with a glass of wine."

Evie looked at the books. They were all romance novels, with cover pictures of manly men and beautiful women lusting for each other. The magazines were updated versions of the ones Sheila and Evie used to read when they lived together in their apartment, full of advice on beauty and fashion, and how to get a man and keep him happy.

Evie started with the magazines. She dieted and exercised until she got her pre-Kathy figure back. She had her hair done at a salon every week, teased at the top and flipped out at the bottom. She learned how to cook delicious meals. She kept up with the news so she'd be an interesting conversationalist.

Nick complimented her on her figure, her hair, her clothes and her cooking. But becoming an interesting conversationalist was a complete waste of time, and they still weren't having any more sex. The magazines were out of ideas.

"Did you read any of the books?" Sheila asked. "They're very good for inspiration."

"What's the point? When we do have sex, I don't feel that connection any more. I'm starting to be glad when he comes to bed late. Sometimes I pretend I'm asleep when I'm not."

"Evie, you always loved sex! You're in very dangerous territory."

Evie sighed. "I know. But I can't pretend I'm interested when I'm not."

"You don't pretend. You do everything you can to become interested. And then you show him."

When Evie arrived home from grocery shopping a few days later, she found a cardboard box tied with a red ribbon and a fancy bow on her doorstep. It was marked "Marriage Survival Kit." Inside were lotions, candles, a black negligee and more romance novels.

She waited until Nick went back to San Francisco. Every evening she put Kathy to bed, she put on the negligee and modeled it in front of the full-length mirror in their bedroom. Then she slipped into bed and read a romance novel as she sipped a glass of wine. Each time, she felt less foolish and more interested.

By the end of the week, she was ready.

Nick had promised he'd be home for dinner and Sheila took Kathy for the night. He was half an hour late. Evie met him at the door and posed in the negligee the way she'd practiced in front of the mirror.

"Surprise," she said. "Sheila's looking after Kathy, so it's just the two of us tonight."

Nick was staring at her in a way that Evie didn't recognize, but she carried on. She took his briefcase and put it on the floor. She put her arms around his neck, leaned into him so her breasts pressed against his chest and reached up to kiss him.

"That's odd." The thought flitted through her mind. "He isn't bending down to kiss me." She reached higher and planted her lips on his. It took some time for his to respond.

Evie was starting to feel disconcerted.

"What do you think?" she asked, posing, but beginning to feel foolish. She could see him struggling with himself. Why?

"You look...very nice, Evie," he said. "But you're taking me completely by surprise. I need some time to catch up."

Catch up? The men in the romance novels never needed time to catch up. She certainly hadn't seen any evidence of him needing to in the past, either.

The rest of the evening was a disaster. Dinner was overdone and cold. So was Evie. Afterward, they walked awkwardly to the bedroom. Evie tried to feel seductive and took off Nick's tie, but he pulled away and took off the rest of his clothes himself.

They lay side by side on the cold sheet until Nick put his arm under her shoulder. She willed herself to feel interested, but it was too late. When it was over, Nick lay on his back. Five minutes later, he got up and went into the den to work.

1959

Kevin was born in March, nine months after Evie's failed seduction of Nick, so in a way it wasn't a failure at all.

As soon as the nurse put him into her arms, Evie knew everything about him. For the first time, she felt like a natural mother.

"I don't understand why Kevin is so easy," she told Sheila a few months later. "I love Kathy, too, but it's so hard for me to feel a connection with her. She still seems like a stranger to me."

"Maybe it's because he's your second," Sheila said, as Kevin beamed his gummy smile at her. "Maybe you don't expect as much from yourself. Or from him."

Nick began taking longer, more frequent trips to San Francisco. He'd promised he'd be home for Kathy's third birthday party in June, but he called Evie that morning to tell her he couldn't get away. When he arrived home the next evening, Evie was ready.

"I understand how important your work is to you," she said, "but it's torture for me to see so little of you. I'm lonely for you all the time." Her eyes started to water. "I need to feel close to you again."

She saw Nick stifle a groan, and she almost heard him thinking, "Not again."

Instead, he reached for her hand. "Evie, you know I love you."

She bit her lip. "No. Not any more, Nick. Do you remember how close we were when we were just starting out? I miss that so much."

"But Evie, we were young. I have responsibilities now. Not just to you and the children, but to Al and my clients."

She let her hand drop to her side. "Are you telling me that you aren't willing to spend even a little more time with us?"

His voice rose. "I can't. Not until—"

"Until when, Nick? As soon as one important case is over, another one comes up. It never ends."

Nick sighed. "Look, Evie, this is supposed to be a part-nership. Please, just take care of the kids and let me do what I have to do."

If she'd felt any connection with him at all, she would have told him, "If you loved us, you'd spend time with us."

Instead, she began complaining about crumbs he left on the kitchen counter, hairs he left in the bathroom sink when he shaved, and dirty clothes he left on the bedroom floor.

"You're overreacting again," he'd say, which infuriated her even more.

"It's never about the crumbs on the kitchen counter," Sheila said when Evie complained to her. "It's just safer to complain about them than it is to talk about what's really the matter."

During the next seven years, Evie stopped thinking of herself as Nick's wife and the mother of his children. Instead she became the wife of a man who came and went, and the mother of two growing children who needed her love.

1966

Evie was cooking dinner and Kathy and Kevin were doing their homework at the kitchen table when Sassy began shaking her head as if she was trying to clear water from her ears. Kevin walked over to pet her.

"Hey, Sass, what's the matter?"

Suddenly, streams of mucus flew from her mouth. Her body twitched from head to tail and she sank to the ground.

"Mom!"

The three of them watched in horror as Sassy's legs flailed against the fl oor. Her eyes were wide with terror. Urine and feces sprayed out, and still she kept jerking. When the spasms finally stopped, her eyes were open and unseeing, and her tongue was hanging out of the side of her mouth.

Evie bent down. "She's breathing."

Evie called the vet while Kathy carried Sassy to the car in a blanket. The two children held her in the back seat.

The vet felt a lump on Sassy's liver and took X-rays. He called the next day to say that Sassy almost certainly had liver cancer.

"We have to have her put down," Evie told the children when they arrived home from school.

"No!" they cried.

"She's over fourteen years old," Evie said. "She's been a good cat and she's had a good life. We have to let her go."

"Daddy wouldn't let you kill her if he was here," Kevin said.

"A lot of things would be different if Daddy was here," Evie said. "But he isn't."

The next morning, Kathy and Kevin sat in front of their breakfast cereal. Evie sat down beside them.

"I'm sorry," Evie said. "I don't want to lose Sassy either, but we're responsible for her and she's suffering. We have to do what's best for her, not for us."

After they left for school, Evie carried Sassy to the vet for the last time. She watched him find a vein in Sassy's leg and inject the poison that would kill her. In moments, Sassy's eyes closed and her body relaxed.

When Evie got back home, Kevin was curled up on the sofa with Sassy's favorite toy. "Why aren't you in school?" Evie asked.

"I never want another cat." He wiped his eyes with his sleeve.

Evie wrapped Kevin in her arms. "I know," she said. "I know."

Chapter Six

Fall, 2001

It's still dark when Nick wakes Evie up. "Time to get up, old girl," he says. "Today's the day."

They move like teenagers, practically bounding down to the garage to get their suitcases. They pull them back upstairs and lift them onto their bed. Nick folds pants, shirts, sweaters, neckties, underwear and socks, and packs them together as efficiently as he did when he traveled for business.

He stops for a moment. Those were the days he felt alive, when he could work all day, every day, and fly to San Francisco at a moment's notice for however long it took to wrap up a deal. He isn't sorry he gave up the San Francisco office for Evie. But still, he misses it sometimes.

He almost lost her once. And now, in spite of all his denials, he knows he's losing her again.

What frightens him the most, though, is that he's also losing his intellect, which he's depended on all his life. It isn't just his memory. He doesn't understand a lot of what he reads in the newspaper anymore. Even when he reads each word out loud and listens to the sound of it, he can't always string them together so they make sense. And if he no longer has that, how can he protect her? He has to get to Edgar and Sheila's. They'll help.

"Nick?" Evie is holding up a wide gold belt. "Should I bring this?"

Her suitcase is overflowing with nighties, slips, scarves.

He forces himself to laugh. "It looks like you're packing for a rendezvous," he says.

When she looks puzzled, he takes everything out and begins again.

"It will probably take two or three days for us to get there, so take three of everything," he says. He goes through her closet and hands her three pairs of long pants, three blouses and three sweaters. When he turns around, he sees that she's jumbled them all together in the suitcase.

"That's good," he says, and he hands her everything else he thinks she'll need. "Now let's make some sandwiches for lunch."

"Oh, Nick," Evie says. "We'll have a picnic."

In the kitchen, Evie places a loaf of bread, sliced meat, lettuce and tomatoes on the counter. She picks up one after the other, examines it and puts it back down. She looks at the muddle as if she's willing it all to fall into place.

"Here," Nick says gently, spreading out the slices of bread and handing her a knife. "Put the butter on first."

But she can't even do that. The knife twists in her hand and half the butter smears onto the counter. "How can you stand me?" she almost wails. "I can't do anything anymore."

"I love you," he says. "We just have to get away from here. Everything will be fine when we get to Edgar and Sheila's."

He puts the sandwiches, some cans of tomato juice from Meals on Wheels, and apples and bananas into a cloth grocery bag. He slides her pill box—the triple-decker, battery-operated one with a woman's voice that reminds them when it's time for Evie to take her pills—into another one.

Until now, Aiden has been giving Evie her pills because Nick turns off the reminder and forgets to give them to her. He throws in all the bottles of pills, too. There's almost no more of her anti-psychotic.

On their way to the garage, Evie looks at the photos covering the door of the fridge. Their children and grand-children smile out at them.

"Who are these people?" she asks. "Why do we have their pictures on our fridge?"

They all came from our life together, he thinks of telling her. They're everything we have ever done that means anything, and we'll probably never see them again.

"Some old friends," he says.

"Oh, yes," she says vaguely.

In the garage, they load up the car. Nick has a flash of a memory of a TV episode he saw recently, where a man escaped from a house by gunning the car in reverse straight through the garage door. A wild feeling catches his heart, but instead, he opens the door with the remote and backs out slowly.

Evie starts to giggle as they turn onto the street. "I wish they could see us now," she says. "The old folks are hitting the road."

Her high spirits are giving him confidence and he begins to enjoy himself.

"Everybody out of the way!" he cries. "We're coming through!"

But when a car honks at them as they weave into the oncoming lane, Nick sobers up. "We have to be careful not to attract attention," he says. "It would be a disaster if we were pulled over."

Evie giggles again. "We'd probably end up in jail. I think I'd like that better than an old folks' home." She puts her hand on his knee. "I know you're doing this for me," she says. "Thank you, dear."

Nick straightens up in his seat. "Stick with me, old girl," he says, his bravado coming back. "I'll take care of you."

When he crosses under the freeway, she looks up in alarm.

"Where are we going?" she asks.

"We have to pick up a prescription for you," he says. "It'll just take a minute."

In the pharmacy, Amit looks at them in surprise. "Hi Evie. Hi Nick," he says. "You on your own today?"

"Aiden's across the street at the doctor's office, making an appointment for Evie," Nick lies.

It's interesting how his sense of himself as an honorable man has changed, he thinks. He used to believe that telling a lie, for any reason, was unforgivable. But now he can no longer afford to tell the truth. Still, he hopes Amit doesn't notice that he's sweating.

Fifteen minutes later, they're on the freeway with their windows wide open. The air is warm for a June morning. Nick's arm is resting on the windowsill and Evie's thin hair is blowing around her face.

"Remember this?" he says. "My dad learned it in Belgium, in the First World War."

He sings at the top of his voice.

> *There are rats, rats,*
> *As big as alley cats*
> *In the stores, in the stores.*
> *There are rats, rats,*
> *As big as alley cats*
> *In the quartermaster's stores.*

And the last verse, quietly, just the way his dad had taught him:

> *My eyes are dim,*
> *I cannot see*
> *I have not got my specs with me.*

And then, Evie joins in, for a rousing

> *I--have--not--got --my--specs--with--me!*

Evie laughs. The asphalt is smooth under their car. The green, rolling landscape speeds by.

> *It's a long way to Tipperary,*

Evie begins, and Nick joins in, his baritone booming out the windows.

> *It's a long way to go.*
> *It's a long way to Tipperary*
> *To see the sweetest gal I know.*

They look at each other, their voices full of the song. When was the last time they were this happy?

> *Farewell, Piccadilly*
> *Farewell, Leicester Square.*
> *It's a long, long way to Tipperary*
> *But my heart's right there!*

Evie leans back in her seat, smiling, her eyes closed. "Sheila and Edgar will be so surprised to see us," she says.

Nick instinctively jams his foot on the brake. "Damn," he says. "I forgot to call them."

The driver behind him leans on his horn and Nick swerves to the right. The car bounces onto the shoulder toward the ditch, but he straightens the wheel just in time. Sweating, he turns off the engine and leans over the steering wheel.

From the corner of his eye, he sees a police car make a U-turn across the median and pull up behind them. He gets out of the car and writes down their license plate number.

Evie looks at him in panic. "He's coming over here!"

"Don't say anything," he says. "Let me handle it."

Evie knows how to do that. Whenever anyone, even their children, start probing about how things are going at the house, she stays as quiet as she can. That's the one thing she's sure of these days.

The officer looks inside Nick's window, first at Nick, then at Evie, who tries to smile but can't quite carry it off, and then at the empty back seat.

"You got a problem, there, folks?" he asks.

"No, Sir," Nick says. "No problem at all, Sir."

"Mind showing me your driver's license and registration?"

"Of course." Nick reaches into the glove compartment and hands over the registration.

"And your license?"

Nick plays for time. "Is there anything wrong, Officer?" he asks.

"You were driving erratically back there."

"I'm sorry. I miscalculated a little when I pulled over."

"I understand. Your driver's license, please."

Nick looks straight into his eyes.

"My son has it, Officer. He doesn't think I should be driving. But my wife's sister is very ill. She lives in Mariposa, just up the road."

"I know where Mariposa is." The officer gives him a hard look. "Is there someone there who can drive you back home?"

"Yes, Officer!" Nick practically shouts. "Thank you, Officer."

"I don't want to see you driving around here again."

"No, Officer. You definitely won't. Thank you again, Officer."

Nick's heart is pounding and fluttering at the same time. He sinks back in his seat. He watches the police car make another U-turn across the divider and speed back toward Sierra Fortuna in a cloud of dust.

"Did I do a good job?" Evie asks.

"Yes, dear. You did a very good job."

Nick careens back onto the road. Evie throws back her head and starts belting out another song:

Daisy, Daisy, give me your answer, do
I'm half-crazy over the love of you.

She falters. Nick is looking straight ahead, his lips tight.

It isn't long before she falls asleep. She's sleeping much more than she used to, Nick worries. He keeps driving for a couple of hours and then exits at a gas station. He slides his credit card into the slot and fills up the tank.

Farther along the freeway, he spots a turnout with picnic tables in a grove of eucalyptus trees. The car rattles off the freeway and into the parking lot. He stops in front of a table.

"Time to wake up, old girl." He gives Evie's shoulder a little massage.

She wakes up with a start. "Where are we?"

"We're on our way to visit Edgar and Sheila, remember?"

"But where are we?"

"We're at a rest stop. We'll have our lunch here."

Evie watches Nick as he spreads out the sandwiches, drinks and fruit.

"You can sit here," he says, and helps her sit at the end of a bench. They face a range of purple mountains beyond a frill of green fields.

"Do you remember the field behind your family's house?" she asks.

"Yes, I do," Nick says.

"I'd like to see your mother again."

His mother would be a hundred and fifteen years old if she were still alive. "She'd love to see you, too," he says.

When they finish their sandwiches, they find the restrooms. The men's and the women's are on opposite sides of a small, square stucco building. Nick toys with the idea of taking Evie with him to the men's side, but he's too old to change his sense of propriety now.

"I'm going to the men's side," he tells her at the entrance to the women's restroom. "If I'm not here when you come out, stay right here and I'll come and get you. Promise me, Evie."

Evie nods. "I promise."

He goes as fast as he can, but on his way back to get her, he finds himself fighting a vague fear. Sure enough, she isn't there. When a middle-aged woman comes out, he asks, "Did you see an older woman in there? With a purple blouse?"

The woman looks surprised, then sympathetic. "No, I'm sorry."

He darts inside. The doors of all four stalls are open.

Nick walks all the way around the restroom building, from the women's entrance across the front to the men's, around the back, and back to the women's entrance again. He checks inside both restrooms a second time, willing her to be there with every step he takes. He goes back to their car, their picnic table. He does a full sweep of the entire parking lot, in between and under all the parked cars, under all the picnic tables, around all the trees, three times.

She's gone.

1969

There was a new girl in eighth grade when Kathy went back to school in the fall, a beautiful, graceful girl with pale white skin, gray eyes and long hair that was so shiny and black that it seemed to have blue highlights. While Kathy and the other girls in town still wore tee shirts and shorts to school, Carole wore a long dress, beads and sandals.

Rumors about her family began before the first class did. Her mother had been a famous singer back East, but her father had gone to jail for dealing drugs. When he got out, the family moved to Sierra Fortuna to make a new start. No, he's an undercover agent for the FBI. No, he testified in a trial and the whole family is in the witness protection program.

Carole sat in front of Kathy in homeroom. They found themselves sitting beside each other in another class, and when it was over, they walked to the lunchroom together. At lunch, Carole told Kathy about the famous artists and musicians her parents knew.

"Want to come to our apartment after school sometime?" Carole asked. "I'll show you the painting Andy Warhol did of my mom."

"I hear there's a new girl in your class," Evie said to Kathy at dinner that evening.

"Carole. Yeah. She's nice," Kathy said.

"Where's she from?"

"I don't know." Kathy looked at Evie through her bangs. "Why?"

"I've heard stories about her parents. And I saw them in the grocery store the other day. Her mother dresses like a gypsy and it looks like she dyes her hair. And her father was in his undershirt. In the grocery store."

"Carole's mom's an artist," Kathy said. "They even have a weird painting Andy Warhol did of her."

Nick stopped chewing.

"Is that right?"

"You went to her house without telling me?" Evie asked.

"Just for a little while," Kathy backtracked. "Did I tell you I'm in the "A" stream in history this year?"

"What did you do when you were over there?" Nick asked.

Kathy's face lit up. "There's a big piano that takes up almost the whole living room," she said. "Maria let me sit beside her and she played songs from the club where she works. She's amazing."

"Maria?" Evie asked. "You call her by her first name?"

"She works in a club?" Nick asked at the same time.

By now, Kathy couldn't stop. "And she sings," she said. "She has pictures of herself onstage when she was young, wearing this slinky black gown and her hair falling down her shoulders."

"Well, that's...uh...different," Nick said. He looked at Evie for help.

She began clearing the table.

Nick stood up and ran his fingers through Kathy's long curls. "You know you can always talk to us about anything," he said.

"Sure, Dad," Kathy said. "Thanks."

Evie was waiting for him in the kitchen. "I told you, Nick. We need you."

What Kathy hadn't told her parents was that Maria painted, too: huge, brightly colored pictures that Kathy couldn't understand.

"That's because they're psychedelic," Carole had explained. "You have to take drugs to see what they are."

"Your mother takes drugs?"

"Sure. Both my parents do. My father's a dealer."

"Wow."

"Next time you come over, I'll show you."

If Kathy's parents had been drug dealers, they'd have told Kathy to stay away from their stuff or else. But the next time

Kathy went to Carole's apartment, Maria told her, "If we told you to stay away from it, that would make you even more curious."

"Anyway, this is only grass," her father added.

That sounded like permission to Kathy. Still, it took her a few more visits before she had the nerve to try it.

Carole took a fat, hand-rolled cigarette from her mother's top drawer, inhaled and lit one of the twisted ends with a gold lighter. The flame burned through the paper and the end flickered red. She held her breath and the red faded. She inhaled, it flickered red, she held her breath and it faded again.

"Here," Carole gasped, and handed it to Kathy.

The instant the smoke hit Kathy's throat, she coughed it back out. "This is so much stronger than cigarettes," she choked. "How do people do it?

"Practice," Carole answered. "Try again."

Through all the coughing, enough smoke made it to Kathy's lungs to have a little effect.

"Look at my mom's painting now," Carole said.

"Oh, wow."

They laughed. They ate. They laughed while they ate. And then it was time for Kathy to go home.

She tried to look as normal as possible as she walked the three blocks to her house, especially because it seemed that everyone she saw was watching her. She focused on taking deliberate steps, all the same length, with her toes pointed straight ahead. This became harder to do when the thought struck her that she couldn't step on any cracks in the sidewalk or she'd break her mother's back. That started her laughing again.

When she finally arrived home, her mother was waiting at the front door.

"Where were you?"

"Nowhere." Kathy tried to edge around her.

"Mrs. Charleton called. She said you were walking very strangely past her house."

Evie sniffed her hair. "Damn those people. I knew it," Evie said.

Kathy didn't know what was more surprising, hearing her mother swear, or that she knew what she'd been doing.

"I'm calling the police. They should both be in jail."

"Mom! No! What would happen to Carole?"

Evie sighed. "All right. I'll wait till your father comes home and see what he thinks. In the meantime, you don't go over there again. Do you understand?"

Evie met Nick at the front door when he returned from San Francisco a few days later.

"Kathy's getting into trouble," she said. "I really need your help."

Nick eased her away from him. "Let me put my suitcase down and relax for a minute," he said. "It can't be that bad."

An hour later, Evie and Nick walked into Kathy's room. Nick sat on the edge of her bed. Evie sat at her desk. She ran her hand across the cool white surface. She and Nick had bought this set of furniture just after Kathy was born. She'd wanted Kathy to have a pink and white bedroom just like the one she'd had before she went to the Girls' Home.

She'd loved that bedroom as a child and she'd always pictured Kathy happy and secure in hers. But Kathy had never wanted or needed the things that Evie had expected her to, and Evie had never felt that she was giving Kathy what she did need.

Suddenly she didn't want to talk to Kathy the way she and Nick had planned. She just wanted to hold her, but she didn't know how to do that, either.

"Kathy," she began. "We love you very much."

Kathy pulled away. "Don't tell me drugs are dangerous," she said. "They already told us all that in school. Besides, it was only grass."

Nick kept to the script. "Fine, we won't. But the fact remains that you're on a dangerous path with this Carole and her parents and we're going to do our best to steer you away from it. If we find that you've gone over there again, we'll call the police. Any questions?"

"That isn't fair! Just because you think they aren't good enough."

"We want you to start babysitting," Evie added. "It's time you took on some responsibility."

"Oh, you want other mothers to trust me with their children when you don't trust me yourself?"

Evie felt a white fury in her chest. "Don't you dare—"

"Dare what?" Kathy yelled. "Since when did you start caring what I do?"

"Evie," Nick said quietly. "Let's go. We're making this worse."

Kathy tried to slam her door as they left, but Evie jammed her foot in the gap to keep it from closing.

"You ungrateful brat. You have no idea how hard I've tried to make you happy. You stay in here until I say you can come out."

Evie pulled her foot out of the way and slammed the door. She jerked it open again and snapped off the light.

"And don't waste our electricity."

Early the next Monday morning, Evie sat on the edge of their bed, watching Nick pack for another trip to San Francisco.

"Please don't go. Not now, when we're having such a hard time with Kathy."

"I have to. You have no idea how much pressure I'm under, and you're making it worse. If I don't keep working like this, the work will stop coming in."

"The work will never stop coming in, and you know it." She touched his shoulder hesitantly. "I know you don't want our kids to grow up poor like you did. But think about the good memories you have of your father, playing ball with you, cooking dinner for you. Kathy's and Kevin's only memories will be of you walking out the door with your briefcase."

"I love you, Evie. Why isn't that enough for you?"

She felt too hollowed out to cry.

"I'm losing the feeling that I'm connected to you. That I can count on you."

Nick looked at her with what might have been great sadness. He snapped his suitcase closed.

"I'm sorry, Evie. I have to go."

"I know he loves me," she told Sheila later. "Why do I need so much more?"

"We think love is all we need to be happy," Sheila said, "but in a relationship, it's just the beginning."

It was about this time that Evie noticed that a small brown mole on the side of her neck had grown to almost twice its size. Lately, she'd started nicking it whenever she put on a necklace. She forgot about it, though, because that afternoon Kathy didn't come home after school.

None of her friends had seen her. There were no activities that Evie had forgotten about, no reasons for Kathy not to be back home except for terrifying ones. Still, Evie waited until dinnertime before she panicked.

Her husband wasn't in his room, the hotel receptionist told her, and no, she didn't know where to reach him. Yes, she would be sure to leave him a message to call his wife as soon as possible. She was very sorry that was all she could do.

Kevin had stopped watching TV. "Maybe she's at Carole's," he said.

Carole. Of course.

Carole answered the door. Her father was in the living room, unshaven and in a sleeveless undershirt. They were both sorry, but they hadn't seen Kathy.

"You could go to the police and report her missing," Carole's father said with such pity that Evie almost broke down.

"The police. Yes. Thank you."

Instead, she drove to Kathy's school and searched the fields in the dark. She cruised the streets for an hour, trying to peer beyond the haze of streetlights, through sinister trees and bushes. She didn't even know what she was looking for. Kathy, staggering drunk, or drugged? Her lifeless body crumpled in a gutter? If she'd been kidnapped and was hidden in someone's back room, how would Evie ever find her?

Evie's hopes rose as she arrived home. Of course Kathy would be back by now. But when Kevin jumped up as she walked through the door, and his face collapsed when he realized that she was alone, Evie knew Kathy wasn't there. Yet, she told herself.

It was after nine o'clock, and dinner was congealing on the kitchen counter. Paperwork that had seemed important a short time ago was a meaningless pile of clutter.

Evie dropped the keys onto the table. "Did Dad call back yet?"

Kevin avoided her eyes. "No."

"I'll go out and look again," Evie said.

"Why don't you go to the police?" Kevin asked.

Evie backed down the driveway not sure where she was going. She just hoped that getting out of the house and doing something, anything, would make the empty feeling in her chest go away. But driving up and down the dark silent streets seemed hopeless. She turned into the parking lot of the police station.

The lobby was lit as garishly as a bus terminal. Two coolers of soft drinks dominated the room. Evie walked up to the desk between rows of people slouched in metal chairs. The young man at the desk looked up.

"My daughter didn't come home from school today. I've called all her friends and no one has seen her."

Evie heard herself say the horror of the words, but she was perfectly calm. She seemed to have separated herself from the mother who had lost her child. She had the totally illogical conviction that she had been caught in someone else's nightmare, and as long as she kept that woman at a distance, she wouldn't break down.

The young man took a few notes and disappeared. While Evie was waiting, a woman stepped up to the desk and asked another young man about her son, who'd been arrested.

Tears pricked at Evie's eyes as her two selves merged for a moment. She realized that she was the bad mother there. This woman's son might be in trouble, but at least she knew where he was. Evie had failed a parent's most crucial responsibility: to keep her child safe.

The young man arrived with a missing persons report. He glanced at Evie to make sure she was ready. They made their way down the list: name, address, height, weight, and then scars, visible dental work. But when he asked if Kathy had ever had a skeletal x-ray, Evie faltered. Who was her dentist, and had she ever had dental x-rays? Had she ever been fingerprinted? Evie began to realize the questions were slanting toward their finding a body, not a child.

Her self-control held, and she answered every one of the horrible questions until the very end, when the deputy turned the paper toward her.

"Will you please sign and date it here?" He pointed to the bottom of the page.

Evie signed her name, but she couldn't remember the date. Could it be January? June? Her mind was blank.

"It's November 14, Ma'am."

She wrote it in and stopped again.

"1969."

"Thank you."

Evie handed the paper back and gathered all her strength. "How do you look for missing people?" she asked.

The young man hesitated, then answered carefully. "There isn't much we can do, Ma'am. Mostly, we wait for someone to see them."

"Wait a minute," Evie wanted to say. "If my daughter is out in public, I don't need you. I need you to make sure she isn't in someone's back room, being murdered. Right now, not tomorrow. You would do something if it were your child."

Instead, she folded her copy of the report. "Thank you," she said.

As she drove back home, she realized for the first time how fragile life really was. The only thing that separated a false alarm from disaster was chance. And the only thing that separated life from death was a heartbeat.

Kevin jumped up, but he collapsed back onto the sofa when he saw his mother's drooping shoulders.

"Did Dad call?" Evie asked.

"No."

He fell asleep with his head on Evie's lap. Evie closed her eyes, and in a few hours, it was dawn. The door opened softly, but they both heard it. Seconds later, Kathy was wrapped up in a tangle of arms.

"I'm sorry," she said, wiping her eyes. "I'm sorry."

Kathy never said where she'd been that night. She stopped seeing Carole, though, and she started seeing her old friends again.

By the time Nick called, a few hours after Kathy had arrived back home, Evie was in a fog of exhaustion and relief.

"I'm sorry I didn't call last night," he said. "My meeting ran late and I didn't get your message until just now. What's the matter?"

Evie was shocked at how little she wanted to talk to him. "It's all right," she said. "We didn't need you after all."

"What happened?"

"Kathy didn't come home last night, but she's back and everything's fine."

"Oh my god. I'll come home right—"

"No. Don't. We're fine."

"But—"

Evie's heart began to thud. "I don't want to see you right now. Stay there and do whatever you have to do. We can talk when you get back."

By the time Nick arrived home, Evie's heartbeats had shifted into a new pattern. She was just as lonely, but her need to feel close to him was gone. She flinched when he tried to kiss her.

"I know I let you down, and I'm sorry, Evie. But—"

"I'm not angry, Nick. You were right. You take care of your life and I'll take care of the rest."

Sheila noticed the coolness between them.

"I can't force him to be someone he isn't," Evie said. "I'm going to do what I have to do for the children. Nothing else matters."

"Not even yourself?" Sheila asked.

"I can wait till they're grown and out of the house."

The next month, the washing machine overflowed. Evie was still in her robe, mopping up the floor when the plumber rang the doorbell. He was new. Tall and good-looking. Heavier than Nick but about the same age.

"Well, hel-lo," he said.

Her hand went to her hair, still uncombed and damp with sweat. She hadn't even brushed her teeth.

"I…," she started. "The laundry room's over here."

She couldn't stop her hips from swaying a little as she led the way.

In the tiny room, he pulled the machine forward. "I'm going to have to squeeze around here to see the back," he said. "Can you hold this?"

He held a flashlight toward her. She let her hand brush his as she took it.

"Just shine it back here."

She reached over him and shone the flashlight on the wires looping on the back as his hands tugged at them one by one. Strong, capable. Short clean nails.

He jiggled the black hose in the back. "Let's give her a try," he said.

Evie pulled the knob. The water gurgled through the hose and down the drain.

"Works every time," he said. "All she needed was the right touch."

His hand barely missed her breast as he took back the flashlight. Evie didn't flinch.

He looked at her for a few seconds too long. "It should be working fine now, but I can come back on Monday to make sure," he said.

"All right," Evie heard herself say.

It was three days of anxiety, guilt and lust. Nick and the children noticed nothing. He had his work and they had their friends. Evie had…what? A stranger who'd promised to whirl her into the mystery of the other, if only for a moment.

The phone rang at ten on Monday morning. "Mrs. Landry? This is Jack from Loring Plumbers."

"Hello."

"Would you like me to come over and check your machine now?"

She could still change her mind.

"Yes. That would be fine. Thank you." As if the formality could erase what she was about to do.

He savored her, caressed her, took pleasure in her pleasure. She hadn't felt as spent and fulfilled for years, and possibly ever, with Nick.

Nick. He lived in a faraway world. Nothing to worry about right now.

Jack kissed her on the cheek at the front door.

"That was great," he said. "Call me if you need any more help."

Evie watched him walk down the path to his truck, the glow fading as her old world came back into focus. The sofa she'd been thinking of replacing, the carpet that needed to be vacuumed. And groceries. She had to get dinner for tonight. And what was she going to tell Nick?

He looked worn out when he arrived home that evening, and for the first time, Evie wondered if she'd been unfair to him all these years.

"How was your trip?" she asked, and without thinking, she began to massage his shoulders. She felt his bones through his white shirt. Fragile. Vulnerable. Her husband.

"We've been having some trouble with a client in San Francisco," Nick said. "A pretty major one."

Her fingers stopped. "Why didn't you tell me?"

"I didn't want to worry you."

"I'd rather worry than feel left out of your life."

He held her hand on his shoulder and kissed it. "Are the kids here?"

"They went to a football game at school. They won't be back for a few hours."

"I'd really like to go to bed with you now."

Oh god.

Evie tried to empty her eyes of the guilt and dread. "I'd like that, too."

They lay on the same sheets where Evie and Jack had lain hours before, on the same mattress, in the same room. Her two worlds collided with a heart-stopping force.

Nick raised his upper body and leaned on his elbow. "What's wrong?"

Evie sat against the headboard. "I cheated on you. I'm sorry."

"What?"

"If only we'd been like this before. It wouldn't have happened."

"What? What are you saying?"

Evie closed her eyes.

"Just…. I'm sorry."

Nick backed away from her. "What the hell did you do? Tell me!"

Shivering, she told him everything.

He shook his head. "No," he said. "No. It can't be. Not you."

"I'm so sorry, Nick. But if you'd…."

"Are you blaming me?"

"No, I'm…." She gave up. "I'm sorry."

Still shaking his head, he turned to face her. "You're sorry? YOU'RE sorry?"

His laugh was ugly. "Do you really think you're the only one who's capable of feeling pain? I work every day trying to give you and the kids the best life I can and you…."

Evie didn't even try to defend herself.

"You never think of anyone but yourself. All you do is whine and complain," he went on. "You selfish bitch."

He stared at her, huddled against the headboard, weeping. "You're pathetic, you know that?"

He opened the closet door, pulled his suitcase from the top shelf and slammed it onto the bed.

Evie jumped.

He threw in clothing, shoes, his shaving kit.

"What—" Evie began.

"None of your damn business," he yelled on his way out the door.

He hadn't touched her, but she felt as if he'd beaten her up.

Chapter Seven

Fall, 2001

Hours after Nick and Evie have left the house for Vancouver, Aiden drives up. The garage door is open and the car is gone. She walks through the garage into the kitchen, where the mess they left remains on the counter: breadcrumbs, scraps of lettuce leaves, the fat trimmed from sliced roast beef.

"Grandma! Grandpa!" Aiden runs through the main floor, takes the stairs two at a time, searches every room. Evie's scarves and nighties are draped across the bed. Their favorite clothes are missing.

She calls Kevin.

"Call 911," he says. "I'll be there as soon as I can."

Within ten minutes, the street is clogged with fire engines and police cars.

Yes, she's sure her grandparents left of their own accord, Aiden tells the officers. No, neither of them has a driver's license. Yes, she can give them the model and year of the car, recent photos and her grandfather's credit card numbers.

"Where do you think they might go?" one asks her.

"Uncle Edgar and Aunt Sheila's," she says immediately. "Their oldest friends. But they live in Canada."

"That's a thousand miles away. Are they capable of going that far?" the officer asks.

"I don't know," Aiden says. "I don't think they could figure out how to get there."

She runs back into the house and brings back the papers and photos for the officers. One of them tells the story to a reporter from a local TV station and holds up a photo of Nick and Evie smiling and holding hands on the patio.

"I want you to contact everyone they know around here," another officer tells Aiden. "Ask if they've seen them or heard from them or if they have any idea where they'd be. We'll call their friends in Canada."

One by one, the vehicles drive off. Aiden walks up the steps into the empty house. She stands in the middle of the cold hall.

"Grandma. Grandpa. Where are you?"

Nick is at the rest stop, hundreds of miles away. Evie could be anywhere.

He runs to the highway and scours it in both directions. If she asked someone for a ride, how will he ever find her? What if she told them that he'd kidnapped her, that he wasn't really her husband, and she wanted to go home? Where would they take her? To a police station. No. That's too terrible to think about.

He tries to quell his panic and think the way she would. Where would she go? What would she want to do? And then he knows. He runs back across the parking lot and almost bumps into a girl. Well, he thinks irrationally, maybe she's a woman, with all those tattoos. Why would a woman....

But then he realizes she's talking to him.

"Are you looking for an old lady?" she's asking.

"An old...," he repeats and nods his head. "Yes. Have you...."

"I saw an old lady running into the field up there." She points behind the restrooms.

Nick's chest hurts. His knee hurts. It's the middle of the day in the middle of the summer and he's sweating. He doesn't want to chase Evie, who probably won't even know who he is.

"Thank you."

He clambers over a rickety three-rail fence and slips on the spears of some dried out weeds. He limps across the field to the shade of an oak tree.

Strange, the path life takes you on. One day, you're a respected former attorney. The next, you're alone in a field in the blazing sun, with torn pants and blood running down your leg. You've lied not only to a police officer, but also to the pharmacist whom you consider a friend. And for what? So you can stay with your wife, who doesn't even recognize you half the time.

He squints at the field. Something is moving, a large purple blur. It's her, now, coming toward him. Not quickly, but happily, he can see it from here.

"I wasn't wandering," she says when she reaches him. "I found a grove of trees, just like I used to play in before I went to the Home. It was so beautiful, I didn't want to leave. Are we going to Sheila and Edgar's now?"

He hasn't seen such a light in her eyes for years. He tries to shake off his fear, his anger, his complete fatigue.

"Yes, dear. I was just coming to get you."

Evie holds onto his arm as they walk out of the field together and shows him where she slipped through a gap in the fence. They lean on each other until they get to the car.

A small crowd has gathered to watch. "Do you think they're okay?" Nick hears someone say.

When he turns on the engine, he sees that it's almost four o'clock. His whole body aches now and what he'd like to do is put his seat back down and sleep until morning. Instead, he steers the car back onto the highway.

Evie is dozing when the announcement comes on the radio. The police are asking for the public's help in finding an elderly couple from Sierra Fortuna. Their car is missing and police believe that the husband, who has a heart condition, is driving. The wife has advanced Alzheimer's. There's a possibility that they're headed for Canada. Their car is a dark blue sedan, license plate....

Nick doesn't even realize the announcement is about them until he hears their license plate number.

"Oh no."

"What?" Evie raises her head to look at him.

"I said it'll be late by the time we find a motel," he says.

"A motel? I thought you were taking me home to Nick."

Oh, no. Not now, please God.

She turns to him. "Who are you? Stop the car and let me out right now!"

"I'm Nick, your husband," he says.

"No, you're NOT!" Evie grabs the wheel and the car swerves onto the shoulder. Nick slams on the brake, and there they are for the second time that day, inches from a ditch. At least there's no police car around this time. Evie is wrestling with the window switch, trying to open the door.

"Let me OUT!" she yells. "I want to see Nick!"

Nick pushes down the childproof lock. He feels the familiar prickling behind his eyes.

Evie pummels his arm and chest and wails for Nick. He can't count the number of times he's willed himself to get through this. This time, though, it feels like something inside has broken. He gathers up all his strength.

"Okay," he says. "I'll take you to Nick."

She calms down immediately. "You promise?" she asks, like a little girl.

He sighs and it seems that his heart floats out of his body along with his breath. "I promise."

He drives straight into the setting sun, but he doesn't try to look away.

It's evening by the time Nick pulls into the parking lot of a tidy motel in Grants Pass. They get out of the car and walk stiffly to the office.

"We'd like a room, please," Nick says.

"Two rooms," Evie says. "This isn't my husband."

Nick flushes. "Evie…"

She raises her voice. "He says he is, but he isn't. We're going to see my real husband." She turns to Nick. "Where is he again?"

"Vancouver," he says, stone-faced.

The receptionist turns to Nick. "Will that be two rooms, Sir?"

"Yes, thank you," he says. "Do you have any adjoining ones?" At least this way he has some chance of hearing her if she leaves her room in the middle of the night.

Evie narrows her eyes. "I'm going to put a chair against my side of the door."

They park outside her room. Nick unlocks the door and pulls her suitcase inside. She closes the door when he leaves and he hears the lock click. He pulls his suitcase into his room and then knocks gently on the adjoining door.

"Do you want to have some dinner?" he asks through the door.

The door opens. "Yes, thank you," she says. She walks ahead of him through his bedroom and onto the path outside, and stops.

"It's this way," he says, pointing to the restaurant next door. They're in the middle of their meal when Evie asks. "Where are my pills? I'm supposed to take pills with my dinner."

Nick swears to himself. He's forgotten about her morning and afternoon pills, too. "You can take them after dinner."

The meal improves her mood. She follows Nick back to the motel and waits while he opens her door. "You'll get my pills?" she asks.

He's already forgotten about them. "Yes, of course."

He opens the adjoining door and tips her evening pills into her hand. She closes the door. He hears the lock click.

Nick lies on the edge of his king-sized bed in the dark. It's probably better this way, he thinks. He gets so lonely sometimes, he can't help touching her, and that's often what sets her off. One minute, she knows she's making love with him and the next, she thinks he's a stranger. That's how he gets some of his worst scratches and bruises.

He feels more than hears her come into the room. She lifts the covers and slides into the bed behind him, not quite touching.

"I'm sorry I'm so much trouble," she says.

He turns around and holds her. "You aren't any trouble."

"Yes, I am," she argues. "Maybe you should put me away."

He smooths her thin hair. "I'll never do that. The day we were married, we put our hands on the Bible and we vowed to stay together till death do us part. That vow is still in effect."

She sighs and snuggles closer to him. "You're a good man, Nick," she says, and soon she's asleep.

1969

Evie cried herself to sleep the night Nick walked out on her. The next morning, she woke up late. Both children were still asleep. She flew into their rooms. Like a witch, she thought.

"Come on, you two, get up. You're going to be late for school."

Kevin stretched. "Where's Dad? Why didn't he wake us up?"

"He left already."

Sooner or later she was going to have to tell them why.

Evie went to see Sheila as soon as the children were out the door.

"Oh, no, Evie. How could you? Why didn't you tell me you were thinking about it?"

Evie bit her lip. "I wanted to do it," she said. "And I was afraid you'd try to talk me out of it."

"Are you crazy? Did you want to destroy your marriage?"

"No," Evie said, "but I've been feeling so lonely. And he paid attention to me. He made me feel special."

"Special," Sheila almost spat. "Most women would kill to be married to a man like Nick. Can't you see that providing for you is the way he shows that he loves you? And if that's not good enough for you, maybe you should let another woman have him. You can live all by yourself and wait until another appliance breaks down so you can feel special with some other random guy who comes by to fix that."

"I don't need you to make me feel worse," Evie said.

"Then what do you need, Evie?" Sheila asked. "Why did you come here?"

"A glimmer of understanding came into her eyes. "Did you do it to get Nick's attention? To punish him?"

Evie raised her eyebrows and half nodded. "Maybe," she said.

"Well, congratulations. Now what?"

Nick knocked on the front door before he opened it that evening. Evie couldn't look at him, couldn't lift herself off the sofa, couldn't breathe.

"I'm just getting a few things," he said.

He was upstairs for a long time, much longer than he needed to slip a few suits and some dry-cleaned shirts into the suitcase he used on long trips. Evie's heart cracked. He must be telling the children.

He stopped at the door on his way out. "I'll come back on Saturday and take the kids out for the day if that's all right with you," he said.

"Of course," Evie choked.

Kevin crept down the stairs and leaned against Evie on the sofa. "Why did Daddy go?" he asked.

"I hurt his feelings very, very badly," Evie said.

"Did you say you were sorry?"

"Yes. But sometimes that isn't enough."

Evie found work as a receptionist at an insurance agency a few weeks later.

"This is harder than I ever thought it would be," she told Sheila. "I send the kids off to school before I catch the bus, but they get home two hours before I do. They call me, but I still worry about them. And by the time I get home I'm exhausted and there's dinner to cook and making sure they've done their homework and getting them to bed on time. I was so frustrated with Kathy the other night that I slapped her in the face."

"Oh, no. Evie. Are you sure you want to do this?"

Evie's face collapsed. "Nick's paying the mortgage and supporting the kids. I can't ask him for more than that. I can't."

She scratched her neck.

"What is that?" Sheila pointed to her neck. "That thing right there. I noticed it a few months ago."

"A mole," Evie said. "I was going to make an appointment to show Dr. Fletcher, but I haven't had a chance."

"I think you should do it soon," Sheila said. "It doesn't look right at all."

The next Wednesday afternoon, Dr. Fletcher looked at Evie's mole through a magnifying glass. "Hmmm," he said. "I'm going to send you to a specialist, just in case."

A week later, Dr. Johansson glanced at it. "Hmmm. I'm going to take a little sample, just in case."

He called in his nurse. He drew a circle around the mole, and they had it sterilized, frozen, incised and bandaged in minutes. It was only when Evie left the office that she realized why.

"There's no point crying, you idiot," she kept telling herself in the taxi on the way home. "Stop feeling sorry for yourself. You don't even know if it's anything to worry about."

She longed to tell Nick. Instead, she made the kids' favorite dinner: hamburger and canned tomatoes mixed with macaroni and cheese.

For the next two weeks, fear about what Dr. Johansson might tell her absorbed Evie's entire being. But somehow a magical space opened up inside the fear and let her carry on with her life. She was more patient and loving with the children and more efficient at work than she'd ever been.

On Wednesday, Dr. Johansson called Evie at work. Her world zoomed in until there was nothing but herself, the doctor and the life-saving phone line between them.

"You have malignant melanoma," he said slowly. "It can spread under your skin and form tumors in other organs. I want you to come in on Friday and I'll take care of it."

When she arrived home from work, she had no memory of what she'd done the entire day. Only one thought filled her mind: "I might die."

"You have to tell Nick," Sheila told her that evening.

"No."

"That's crazy."

"Please, Sheila."

"Then I'll tell him."

"No! I can take care of this myself."

Sheila drove her to Dr. Johansson. He carved out a large circle of skin down the side of her neck, sewed the edges together and taped a bandage over the stitches.

"I'll have the results back in about three weeks," he said. "I'll call you and let you know if I got it all."

An hour later, Evie was lying on the sofa waiting for the children to come home from school. The door opened and Nick burst in.

"Sheila just told me. Are you okay?"

Evie tried to sit up. "Yes, I—"

"Why didn't you tell me?"

"I just didn't.... Oh, Nick, I'm so scared."

He reached her before she could stand.

"I'm so sorry," she cried into his chest. "I'm so sorry."

He stroked her hair. "Shhh. I know. I know. It was my fault, too."

"No. I took the easy way out. I'm so sorry."

He sat beside her and wiped her eyes. "So, what are we going to do?" he asked.

"Can you come back home and try to trust me again?"

He stroked her hand. "Of course. I was getting tired of that motel room anyway."

"Oh, Nick."

He held up his hand. "But I have to warn you that I still might not be home as much as you want."

"I understand that."

"And if I'm not, will you believe that I'm doing my best?"

"Yes."

"Okay, then."

He ran one finger around the bandage on her neck.

"Can I see it?"

Gently, he peeled back two of the adhesive strips and lifted up the bandage. The gash was two inches long, with swollen white edges and a line of scarlet blood between them. A row of Xs crudely sewn with thick black thread bound the edges together.

Evie raised her hand to cover it.

He kissed her lips. "You're going to look like a woman of mystery," he said. "Everybody's going to wonder what kind of lover's quarrel that came from."

She leaned against him.

"Why don't you go to bed? I'll take care of the kids when they get home."

Evie lay in bed for a long time remembering the times they'd been happy. When she woke up, Nick's side of the bed was rumpled.

Nick called Evie at work that morning. "How are you feeling?"

"I'm fine. Why'd you leave so early this morning?"

"I had things to do," he said. "Do you feel like going out after work this evening?"

"Where?"

"It's a surprise. Wear long pants and a jacket."

Evie called Sheila. "Are we still friends?" Sheila asked.

"The best. Thanks, Sheila. Do you think you could look after the kids this evening? Nick asked me to go out with him."

"I'll keep them overnight if you like. In case you have any plans."

When Evie stepped outside that evening, she saw a big black motorcycle parked at the curb. She couldn't help laughing.

"Where did you get that?"

Nick grinned. "I borrowed it from a client."

And just like in the old days, she climbed on behind him and held him tight. They rode all the way to their beach. The rutted dirt road had been paved with asphalt, and instead of fields, pretty cottages lined both sides. But the same sandy path led to the same cliff, although it had eroded considerably since the last time they'd been there.

They sat with their backs against the cliff.

"Do you remember the first time you brought me here?" Evie asked.

"I remember everything."

"We were so naive. We had no idea...."

He held her hand between his two and kissed it. "I knew I wanted to be with you."

"But you didn't realize how much of you I'd need."

"No. I didn't."

She was silent.

"It was never because I didn't love you," he said.

"I know."

They huddled against each other the way they used to. Wispy clouds obscured the moon, exposed it in all its translucent glory and obscured it once again. Stars that had been extinct for millennia glittered like diamonds in their vast black velvet jewelry box, and the inky water lapped at the sand, pulling invisible grains back into the bottomless ocean.

He nudged her awake. "Ready to go home?"

He offered her his hand and pulled her up. They climbed the sandy path and rode home, Evie leaning against his back and inhaling the smell of him.

She unlocked the front door and held it open for him.

The next morning, she woke up as he was getting out of bed. He lay back down and put his arm around her. "I'll make us breakfast. Since you're injured," he said.

"Don't you have work to do?"

"It can wait."

She raised herself up on her elbow. "Is this some kind of temporary insanity?"

"It's more a sign of things to come."

Evie's insides began to tingle. She leaned toward him. Their lips met. But just when she felt him lean into her, he pulled back.

"How long can Sheila keep the kids today?"

"I don't know. For the rest of the morning, probably. Why?"

"If I go back to my motel room now, can you come in about half an hour?"

"Why?"

"I have another surprise for you."

Half an hour later, Evie knocked on Nick's door. The door opened, and there he was, grinning and shirtless with a rope around his waist. A cluster of oblong balloons hung from the rope like a bouncy, multi-colored grass skirt. In his right hand, he held up a pin.

"What do you think?" he asked. "I thought we could do something different to celebrate."

"Oh, Nick." Evie burst out laughing.

He looked confused and hurt.

"Oh, Nick," she tried again, but she burst into laughter again.

"But I've been planning this," he said. "I thought you'd like it. Look." He popped a few balloons and moved seductively toward her.

She caught herself mid-laugh and tried to hug him, but some balloons were still in the way.

"Just a minute," he said, and he popped a few more. She held him, laughter still welling up inside her.

"I love you," she said.

The drought began the next year. Lawns were the first to go, and then the flowers from imagined gardens back East: roses, daisies, lily of the valley. Through the next four years, trees that had weathered previous droughts dropped their brittle leaves and died. For the first time anyone could remember, coyotes began to nest in the town instead of coming down from the hills at night in search of food and water.

1974

The temperature was so high the afternoon Evie opened the door for the mailman that the doorknob was hot. She signed for the packet from Elizabeth Stockton, her parents' old friend in Mariposa, and stood under the ceiling fan to read it.

> *My dear Evie,*
>
> *Your father asked me to send you these photos. I understand that you aren't close, but I wanted to tell you that he's still very weak from the pneumonia and if you'd like to see him, you should come as soon as you can.*
>
> *All my love,*
> *Elizabeth Stockton*

The envelope fell from Evie's hand.

Kevin found her sitting on the floor, sifting through glossy black and white photos. He picked one up. "Who are these people?" he asked

"They're my parents, your grandparents," Evie said, "and me when I was a girl."

"Kathy!" he yelled up the stairs. "Come and see some old pictures of Mom!"

Kathy's door opened a crack. She went down the stairs and watched them. Soon she joined them on the floor.

Evie pointed to the tall, thin, fair-haired man in one of the photos. "This is my father," she said. "And this," she pointed to the pretty woman with dark permed curls, "was my mother."

And there was Evie, as a baby being held by her father, as a little girl with straight brown hair sitting on a rock at the beach, and as a preteen standing in front of a brand new blue and white station wagon, squinting into the sun.

In some of the photos, Evie's father and mother were smiling at each other and at the photographer. In another, her mother was holding little Evie's hand and barely smiling at all.

Kathy stroked one of the photos, of a five-year-old Evie hugging a little brown dog and her parents watching in the background. So this was where her mother came from: the kind-looking man and the beautiful mother.

"You never talk about your parents," Kathy said.

"I never really knew them," Evie said. "Especially my mother. I used to think she didn't love me, but now I think she just didn't know what I needed from her or how to give it to me. I didn't realize that until it was too late."

Evie caught her breath and turned to Kathy. Their eyes met—in Kathy's, a question, in Evie's, a realization.

"Oh god," Evie said.

She rushed to Kathy. They hugged awkwardly at first, not sure how close to get or where their bodies fit together. Gradually, they both relaxed and for the first time they felt the softness between them.

"What's going on?" Kevin asked.

"It's fine, Sweetie," Evie said, wiping her eyes. "I think everything is fine, now."

That night, Evie lay in Nick's arms and told him what had happened.

"Children need so much from their parents," she said. "How can any parent not fall short?"

Elizabeth Stockton had included her phone number. She answered on the first ring.

"My dear," she said, "I'm so glad you called. I was about to call you. I'm very sorry, but your father passed away last night. I hope you can come to the funeral. If you want to, you can meet us here at your father's house."

Evie had never been able to force her fingers to dial his number. She could never separate her love for him from the pain she felt whenever she thought of him. And now he was gone. And it was too late to tell him she loved him, to show him his grandchildren, to allow him into her family.

She couldn't cry, for herself or for him. If she did, she would never stop.

Three days later, Evie left for her father's house in Mariposa.

"You're sure you don't want me to come with you?" Nick asked again.

Evie kissed him on the cheek. "No, thanks, darling. I'll be fine. You stay here with the kids."

She almost drove past the house with its bright white walls and turquoise door. In spite of the drought, oranges and avocados hung from the trees. There were three cars in the driveway.

Evie rang the bell hesitantly. A boy about five years old flung open the door.

"Are you Evie?" he asked.

More children clustered around the door.

"Let her in, for goodness sake," someone called from the living room. "And it's Mrs. Landry to you."

The children led Evie to the living room. It was bright now, with light-colored walls and blue flowery drapes. A blue corduroy sofa and love seat with plump cushions had replaced her parents' sad old furniture. Eight adults stood up and introduced themselves one by one as Elizabeth Stockton's children and their spouses. The nine children playing cards on the carpet were her grandchildren.

Still no thoughts had formed in Evie's mind when Elizabeth Stockton appeared in an apron, holding a dishtowel.

"Evie, my dear, I'm so glad you made it," she said. "Why don't you come into the kitchen and we can have a cup of coffee?"

All the old appliances were there, shinier than Evie had ever seen them. The walls were papered with bold-colored fruits and vegetables.

Elizabeth Stockton sat across the oak table from Evie. "I suppose you'd like to know what's been going on in your father's house."

She took a breath. "After your mother died, I began doing little things for your father. Bringing him meals, doing his laundry. Keeping him company. We became very fond of each other, and eventually we became very...close."

Elizabeth Stockton's eyes began to water. "Your father was very kind to my children and grandchildren. I think he liked having them around."

"I've been feeling so guilty for not visiting him with my children," Evie said.

"He would've loved that. There were many times he wanted to call you, but he wanted the choice to be yours. He felt guilty, too."

"I wish—" Evie began.

Elizabeth Stockton put her hand on Evie's. "Are you happy?" she asked.

Evie nodded. "Yes. I am."

"Then that's all that matters."

The older woman paused for a moment. "Your father left me this house. I never intended to take anything away from you, my dear. I hope you don't feel I have."

Evie bit her lip. "You must have been very kind to him," she said.

"He was a very good man. We'll miss him."

They held hands across the table, their faces wet with tears.

Kathy had managed to graduate from high school that summer, but she'd refused to go to university. Nick and Evie drove her to the bus terminal on a suffocating morning. They sat on one of the walnut benches while they waited for her bus.

"At least San Francisco will be cooler," Nick said.

"You're sure you have the address of the youth hostel?" Evie asked again.

The bus pulled into one of the bays and Kathy heaved her backpack and her guitar over one shoulder.

"I'll be fine." She kissed them. "I promise I'll call."

Evie hugged her one last time. "We'll always be here for you," she said.

For the next few years, every time Kathy went back to visit her parents she was happy. In San Francisco, she rented a room in a house where she shared food and chores with ten others. She waitressed at a restaurant on Fisherman's Wharf. She worked at a community day care center, at a department store. She walked dogs.

"When are you going to start going to university?" Nick asked every time she visited them.

"As soon as I'm ready," Kathy always answered.

1977

In the spring, Kathy told her parents that she was taking two classes at Berkeley: psychology and sociology."

"Well, those will do you a lot of good," Nick said.

"Nick. Since when have you been so negative?" Evie asked. "Just be glad she's finally going."

"I am," he said. "I just—"

"Want her to be happy," Evie finished for him. "Then let her do what she wants."

"Hmmph. Fine."

Kathy looked at her father until he broke into a smile.

"Okay," he said. "You win. As long as you keep coming back to visit us."

Kevin graduated from high school that summer and went north, too, to the University of California in Davis, which had one of the best veterinary colleges in the state.

After waving goodbye to him, Evie turned to Nick. "It's just you and me again," she said.

Nick looked at her and grinned. "I know what we can do."

"I'll beat you upstairs!"

A few weeks later, Sheila told Evie that she and Edgar were moving to Vancouver to be closer to their daughter Sophie and her family.

"I'll...I'll miss you," Evie said.

"Who was that?" Nick asked after she hung up.

"Sheila. She and Edgar are moving to Vancouver."

"Oh, Evie. I'm sorry."

"It's just, on top of Kathy and Kevin being away.... We don't even have a cat anymore."

"We can visit everyone, you know. And we can get another cat if you want one."

"You know you're too busy to take time off."

"Not if I cut back and work just a few days a week. Al's son has been wanting more responsibility, anyway."

Chapter Eight

Fall, 2001

On the second morning of their escape, Nick and Evie drive slowly down the main street of the town. They pull into a gas station and Nick slides a credit card into the slot at the bay. As he watches it disappear, he feels a tug on his heart. He's been leaving a trail of credit card purchases behind them.

"We have to find a bank and get as much cash as we can," he tells Evie once he's back in the car.

They drive up and down the main street again, looking for a branch of their bank. Evie is the one who spots it. She may have Alzheimer's, but she's still the better navigator. Nick withdraws $200 from the ATM and they careen back onto the freeway, heading north.

"Are we almost there?" Evie asks.

"No. Tomorrow sometime, probably."

They pass a freeway sign that shows that Eugene, Oregon is almost a hundred and fifty miles away. They might be able to make it that far by lunchtime, Nick thinks. Vancouver seems enormously far away all of a sudden, too far to comprehend.

He drives on, hyper alert for highway patrol cars and any other car that comes too close, all the while trying to pretend that everything is just fine.

Evie passes the time by looking out the window and commenting on the scenery. "Aren't the mountains beautiful up here," she says, and "Oh, look. The cows are all facing the same direction. It's going to rain," and "There's a white horse, and I can't see his tail. Quick, make a wish."

"I wish we were already there," Nick says. His eyes are burning with the strain and his head is starting to ache.

"What?"

"I said, I forgot to call Sheila and Edgar again," he says.

"Look! A market! Let's get something for lunch."

Nick swerves into the exit lane and down the off ramp into the parking lot. "We'll go in in a minute," he says. "I have to call Sheila and Edgar first and tell them we're coming."

He rummages in the glove compartment until he finds the cell phone Kevin gave him. Kevin has explained to him, many times and always very patiently, how to use the phone. He's also put Sheila and Edgar's phone number somewhere inside it, so all he has to do is find it, but Nick has always secretly believed that it would never work without Kevin there.

How can it be possible to make a telephone work just by touching a picture on the screen? It defies any logic that he's equipped to understand.

He remembers to turn the car engine on and plug the wire dangling from the phone into the circle for the cigarette lighter. He pushes every button he can find and swipes his finger in all directions across the screen until suddenly it's filled with tiny, unfathomable pictures. He touches them at random. They slide across the screen and out of view, or enlarge momentarily, or expose something else unrecognizable underneath. He finally notices something that looks like a telephone receiver and stabs desperately at it until it, too, disappears.

"Goddamn it," he swears to himself, but loudly enough for a teenager in a backwards baseball cap to stop as he walks by the car window.

He pokes his head through the open window. "Need help?" he asks.

"Thanks," Nick stammers. "I want to call my friend."

"What's his name?"

Nick tells him. The teenager reaches through the window, taps the screen a few times and hands the phone back. It's ringing.

"Thank you!"

The teenager grins and skateboards off.

"Nick!" Edgar's voice booms out. "Where are you? The police have been here looking for you."

Of course. He should have realized that. "You know us, Edgar," he tries out. "We're just out for a little drive."

"Well, I'm surprised they haven't tracked you down yet. Your pictures are all over the news, your license plate, everything. Your kids are worried to death. They've even been on TV asking you to go to the nearest police station."

Oh no.

"Are you still there?"

"Edgar, I can't talk any more right now. But if Evie and I can make it to your place, could we stay with you for awhile?"

"Of course," Edgar says. "As long as you like."

Inside the market, Nick and Evie choose two homemade meat pies still warm from the oven and pick up two bottles of ice-cold apple juice. While they're in line at the check stand, Nick realizes that his car, and the license plate, are visible to anyone driving along the road.

"Evie," he says, "I have to move the car. Can you stay here and pay for our lunch if you get to the front of the line before I come back?"

"Of course I can," she says. "What do you think is wrong with me?"

He hands her the basket and a twenty dollar bill, moves the car to the row closest to the market, in front of an SUV, and hurries back inside. Evie is trying to pull the bill away from the checker. A long line has formed behind her.

"What's the matter?" he asks.

"He's trying to take our money."

"It's all right." Nick gently takes the bill from her and gives it to the checker, who, expressionless, hands him the change.

"I'm sorry," Nick apologizes to no one in particular.

"It's no problem," says a heavyset woman behind them. "My mother's like that, but not as bad."

"What did she say?" Evie asks, as Nick hustles her out the door.

"She was asking for directions," he says.

"It didn't sound like…"

Nick opens the car door for her. "Let's go and find a nice quiet spot to eat," he says.

"Look." She points to a shady area beside the market. "There are picnic tables right there."

"We'll find a much better place."

Instead of turning back onto the freeway, he follows a narrow road alongside it. For about a mile and a half, he drives more carefully than he has since his children were babies. He spots a dirt road and takes it up to a shabby green metal building.

"This looks like a good spot," he says, as the car bumps over the ruts and comes to a stop.

"But there's nowhere to sit, and we're right beside this ugly building," Evie protests.

Nick opens the windows. "There," he says. "Now we have a nice breeze."

There is a breeze, and a constant hum of insects from the fields on both sides of the car. They sit with their paper napkins on their laps, eating with their meat pies in one hand and plastic forks in the other.

"We could stay here tonight," Evie says. "We could sleep in the field. Do you remember…?" Her voice trails off.

"The time we wanted to go camping and we couldn't find the campground? We ended up sleeping in a field and we woke up with a herd of cows staring at us."

"Oh Nick," she said. "We used to have so much fun."

"Yes, we did."

"And now look. I can't even eat properly. My wrist won't turn."

Instead, she's trying to bend her body sideways to meet her plastic fork. Crumbs litter her slacks and dark streams of juice from the meat streak her blouse.

"Here," Nick says, turning toward her. He takes a forkful of her pie and raises it to her mouth. She leans forward and opens her mouth like a baby bird.

Once they're back on the freeway, Evie sleeps for hours. Nick shifts in his seat, tries to stretch his legs, tries to keep his burning eyes from closing for too long, prays for a miracle.

He watches his speed obsessively, not too fast or too slow, and makes sure he keeps plenty of distance between his car and the one in front. And then he spies the telltale colors of a highway patrol car behind him on the left. It's gaining on him.

There's an exit not too far ahead. Nick resists the urge to speed toward it. Instead, he waits until almost the last second and swerves onto the off ramp.

"What happened?" Evie mumbles.

"Nothing. Go back to sleep."

He stops at a red light and spies a big rig across the street, parked between a gas station and a restaurant. When the light turns green, he cuts across the lane and parks beside it, out of view of the street. He lets out a deep breath and leans back. He's sweating so badly that his shirt is stuck to his seat.

He waits and waits. Enough time for the patrol car to turn at the next exit and come back and search the streets for him. Enough time for his heartbeats to slow down. Enough time for Evie to wake up again.

"Where are we?" she asks.

"I don't know exactly. I thought a patrol car saw us so I got off the freeway."

"Why are you afraid of a patrol car?"

"Because...."

Evie leans toward him.

"Why?"

"Because the police are looking for us. Don't you remember?"

"The police?"

"Everyone wants to put you in a nursing home. That's why we're going to Sheila and Edgar's. Don't you remember?"

Evie cocks her head. "But they live in Canada."

Nick inhales and holds his breath.

"Yes," he finally says. "They do."

"I'd rather die," she says. "I'd rather be killed in a car crash than go into one of those places."

"You won't be killed in a car crash and you won't be put in a home," Nick says. "I won't let anything happen to you."

That was the problem. It was one thing to promise that he'd look after her when he was in his twenties, or thirties, or sixties. But what could he do to protect her now, besides keep running? And how long could he do that for?

It had been futile from the beginning, he realizes now. Even if they did get to Sheila and Edgar's, what would happen then? Evie was never going to get better. He might as well just give up now. It would be a relief, really.

He feels her take his hand.

"Thank you, dear," she says, looking into his eyes. "I picked a good man when I picked you."

"Evie? Do you know who I am?"

"Of course. You're Nick. My husband."

He starts the engine and turns the car around. "Then let's get going."

1978

Nick semi-retired in January, just as the rain started coming down. He and Evie adopted a dog, a little brown and black mutt one of their neighbors found under his hedge one wet day. He took it to Nick and Evie, still muddy and shivering in an old towel.

"I thought of you two right away," the neighbor said. "Your house has been awful quiet since the kids left."

"Thanks, George." Nick's voice was rough. He took the bundle and Evie stroked the long, thin ridge on the dog's head.

"Well," Nick said, as he dried the dog in the kitchen and Evie poured some milk into a bowl. "Here we go again."

The dog looked at them with soft scared eyes. Her hipbones jutted out, her short curly fur was wet and matted, and her scrawny tail disappeared between her stubby legs. Still, there was something about her.

"She's going to be beautiful," Evie said. "Let's call her Gracie."

Nick, Evie and Gracie settled into a happy routine.

Nick and Evie went grocery shopping together and Nick started cooking for the first time since he'd been a bachelor. Soon he was making bread and homemade soup. Evie began volunteering at the local library. They both joined a seniors' group and made new friends.

Evie's favorite part of the day, though, was her morning walks with Gracie. She'd walk up the hill to the park, where she'd sit on a bench and watch the children play. If she wanted to take the long way home, she'd head west, toward the freeway and through one of Sierra Fortuna's last pieces of undeveloped land, five acres of walnut trees.

1981

When Kevin graduated from the university in Davis in the spring, Evie and Nick drove up for his graduation. He'd been accepted into their School of Veterinary Medicine and was still working part-time cleaning the cages at an animal shelter. He was renting a one-bedroom house that he shared with a dog he'd adopted from the shelter, a shy mutt with short caramel-colored fur, floppy ears and long skinny legs.

Evie looked around the bare living room. "You aren't lonely?"

He stopped scratching the dog for a moment. "No, Ma. We're good for now."

"Okay, son," Nick said. "Just let us know if you need anything."

They drove back up to Berkeley that August to celebrate Kathy's graduation with a Bachelor's degree in psychology, seven years after she'd graduated from high school. That was when they found out she had a boyfriend.

Kathy opened the door to her apartment, wearing a long skirt and a peasant blouse with a clunky turquoise necklace. A smiling young man came into view behind her, with almond eyes, a scraggly black beard and copper-colored skin.

Evie and Nick raised their eyebrows at each other.

"Mom, Dad. This is Mark." Kathy's eyes glowed.

Mark shook their hands. "I'm very pleased to meet you."

Evie looked at Nick.

"Well," Nick began. He looked at Evie.

"Please come in," Mark said.

There'd been changes in the living room since Evie and Nick had been there six months before. A glossy black electric piano took up most of one wall. A guitar leaned against the sofa. A different sofa.

Evie pointed to the piano. "Is that yours, Mark?" she asked too brightly.

"The piano? Yes."

"Do you play it?"

"Yes."

Silence.

Kathy came back from the kitchen and put her arm through Mark's. "Mark's a fabulous musician," she said.

"A magician? How interesting," Evie said.

"Mu-sician," Kathy corrected.

"Oh, of course. I...."

Nick put his arm around Evie's shoulder. "I'm afraid we're both a little taken aback," he said.

Mark looked at Kathy. "You told them?"

"Not yet."

"Told us what?" Nick asked.

"Let's talk during lunch," Kathy said. "I'll be right back." And she ducked into the kitchen.

"I'll give you a hand." Mark followed her in.

A few minutes later, he set up a card table in the living room and laid out plates of soy sauce chicken, vegetables and rice.

"Please," he said. "Help yourselves."

They ate in silence.

"This is delicious, isn't it?" Evie finally asked Nick.

Nick stopped eating for a moment. "Yes. It is."

More silence.

"Did you make it?" she asked Mark.

"Kathy did," he said. "She's a good cook."

"I'm glad you like it," Kathy said.

More silence, so deep that Evie could hear herself swallow.

"Mark plays the guitar, too," Kathy burst out. "He's amazing."

"We play together," Mark said. "Did you know Kathy writes her own songs?"

"No," Evie said. "We didn't."

Knives and forks scraped plates.

"So," Kathy said. "I guess I should tell you that Mark and I are living together."

"No kidding," Nick said.

Evie looked from one to the other. "How long have you been...uh...?"

Kathy looked at Mark and blushed. "A couple of weeks," she said. "We met in January."

"In January," Nick repeated. "A whole...what? Six months?"

"And a half."

"Are you planning to...uh...get married?" Evie asked.

"Mom!"

"We're very serious about each other, Mrs. Landry," Mark said.

Nick turned to him with the chilling look he'd used when the children were young. "I'm glad to hear that."

Now Evie couldn't swallow at all.

Kathy nodded toward Mark. "Tell them what you're doing."

Mark cleared his throat. "I'm starting my PhD in Math next month. I decided it's more practical for when I have a family. I can still play music for fun."

"How do you plan to support my daughter while you're getting your degree?" Nick asked.

"They're going to take me on full time at the clinic as a receptionist," Kathy said.

Nick swiveled around to her. "You're going to—"

"Nick." Evie touched his arm. "This is 1981, not 1951."

"You aren't a women's libber, are you?" Nick asked. "How liberated is it to work full-time and take care of a house, too?"

"We won't be able to afford a house for awhile," Mark said.

"Mark already helps," Kathy said at the same time.

Nick's face dropped. "You do?"

Mark's face was hard to read.

"Of course he does," Kathy said.

Nick shook his head. "Well, we'll see."

"What kind of work do you see yourself doing with a PhD?" Evie asked. "Will you teach?"

Mark's face lit up. "I'm going into computer software development," he said. "I'm working with a friend in his garage on a game that will run on a personal computer. They're the next big thing. Ten years from now, almost everyone will have one."

Evie grinned at Nick. "Is that right," she said.

Nick shook his head. "I'll be interested in hearing how it goes."

Mark stood up and started clearing the dishes. Evie followed.

"I'll do them," he said. "Stay here and have a nice talk with Kathy."

Kathy sat on the sofa between her parents. "Isn't he wonderful?" she sighed.

"He certainly seems to be," Evie said. "How did you meet?"

"He was playing his guitar on the steps of the library one evening," she said. "I don't know what made me do it, but I sat down beside him and started to sing with him. We've been together ever since."

"Do you think you'd ever want to move closer to home?"

"We thought about it," Kathy said, "but there's more opportunity for Mark up here. It isn't that far. We'll visit you."

And so it goes, Evie thought.

1982

The next time Nick and Evie drove up, it was for Kathy and Mark's wedding. They met Kevin and his new girlfriend at the hotel restaurant in Berkeley. Kevin was smiling as if he'd won the prize of a lifetime, a slim girl with curly black hair and skin the color of coffee with a few drops of cream.

"My kids are going to kill me," Nick muttered to Evie.

Evie pressed his hand. "Remember where you got your hair from," she whispered.

"Mom. Dad," Kevin said. "This is Chela."

Chela had a lopsided smile that made Evie want to hug her.

"Hello," Chela said, with her crooked smile and straight white teeth. "I've been looking forward to meeting you. Kevin's told me so much about you."

Evie smiled back.

Chela and Kevin had met the day they began vet school. She'd grown up on a ranch in Chino, in the hot, dry Inland Empire east of Los Angeles, with her parents and four brothers and sisters. All the children had helped with the animals—horses, sheep and chickens.

"She delivered her first lamb when she was twelve," Kevin said, "in the middle of the night."

"And I had to go to school the next morning," Chela laughed.

Nick nodded. "I think I'd like your parents, my dear," he said.

The next day, Nick and Evie drove Kevin and Chela to Kathy and Mark's apartment.

The moment she stepped inside, Evie had a flashback to the day Sheila had married Edgar. Boxes of gifts overflowing with colored tissue paper, clothing strewn over the furniture, half eaten meals on plates on the tables.

She sat heavily on the closest chair, listening to the excited voices around her, stunned at what had come of her life.

She'd been so much younger than these children when she was their age, innocent about men and women, love and the birthings of lambs. And this noisy, happy family had come from her, in all her struggles. Her husband, her children, their loves. The world had been going on and she'd been part of it all along, even when she'd felt the most alone.

She looked down at her lap and saw dark splotches spreading on her dress as tears slipped down her cheeks. She felt a hand on her shoulder.

"Mom, are you okay?"

Her beautiful Kathy in her wedding gown, looking at her with concerned eyes. Whoever would have thought that red-faced, squalling baby, that rebellious teenager, could have grown into such an exquisite young woman. Not Evie, that's for sure.

And then Kevin was leaning toward her, and Mark and Nick and Chela.

"What is it?" they asked. "What's wrong?"

Evie looked at them, one by one. "I love you all," she said.

Chapter Nine

Fall, 2001

Nick stays on the frontage road. They pass forlorn auto repair shops and bars, small, shabby houses, and weedy lots surrounded by chain link fences. Every few miles, an intersection with fast food restaurants and gas stations crops up, along with a sign pointing to a freeway onramp. Then the road leads away from the freeway and curves so many times that Nick loses all sense of direction.

"It's that way." Evie points to the left, and soon they're on a freshly paved road that passes a new development of sandy-colored stucco houses behind eight-foot block walls. They pass at least one mini-mall, and sometimes two or three, at almost every intersection.

Evie becomes agitated again. "Where are we meeting my father?" she asks. "I don't recognize anything around here."

"We aren't meeting him today," Nick says, hoping for the best. "I think it's tomorrow."

"No. It's today. I'm sure of it. Where are we meeting him?"

"I don't know, Evie. He didn't tell me."

"Nick."

"I can't, Evie—"

She wrestles with her seat belt, trying to get loose.

"Evie. Stop—"

The car swerves as Evie punches Nick's arm.

"Let me out!"

"Evie, just wait. Okay, we're going to meet him in here."

Nick swings into a mall and finds a coffee shop.

"I don't see him," Evie says as soon as they walk in. "Where is he?"

"Quiet, Evie. Everyone is looking."

"I don't care. I want my father."

Nick can barely stop himself from screaming, "Your father is dead!" Instead, he says mildly, "Why don't you sit down. I'll get coffee for all of us."

Evie is pacing in front of the picture window when Nick returns.

"Come and sit down," he says. "We'll wait for him here."

Evie sips the coffee and they share a homemade pastry with a crisp, light crust and raspberry filling.

"This is very good," she says, "But where's my father?"

"Maybe he couldn't make it." Nick says. "We can call him when we get to Sheila and Edgar's."

"Can we go now?"

"Sure. Do you want to go to the restroom first?"

He opens the door for her and then rushes back to the counter. "Is there another way out of there?" he asks.

The girl behind the counter looks at him strangely. "No."

Almost as soon as they're in the car, Evie's head nods forward. She's asleep.

Nick leans back and closes his eyes. His skin is tingling from the strain of driving and having to coddle her, as well as the fear of being caught. It's hopeless. He has no idea where they are or how to get to the Canadian border. And even if they got there, he now realizes, how could they possibly cross it? Suddenly, he's exhausted.

He wakes up with a start. A middle-aged woman in a flowered blouse and turquoise shorts is knocking on his window. He has to turn the engine on to open the window, and that wakes up Evie.

"Where am I?" she says. "I want to go home."

"Are you okay?" the woman asks Nick.

"Who is that woman?" Evie asks.

"Yes," Nick says. "We're fine. Thank you."

"Who is she?" Evie asks again.

"I'm sorry to bother you, dear," the woman says, "but I was just passing by and I wanted to make sure you were both all right."

"Yes," Nick says again. "We were just resting for a moment."

"On a long trip, are you?"

"Not really," Nick says, on alert suddenly.

"Yes, we are," Evie says. "We're going to visit our friends in Canada."

"Canada," the woman says. "Say, you aren't those folks everyone is looking for, are you?"

"No," Nick says.

She looks into the back seat of the car. "Uh huh. Because if you were, I might be able to help you."

"How?" Nick asks.

"They're looking for your car, but they aren't looking for mine."

"You'd do that?"

"Tell you what. I live right near here. Why don't you follow me back to my place. I'll ask my husband if it's all right with him."

Her friendly eyes have become beady, and they look too eager in her wide, red face. Nick has an immediate impulse not to trust her, but it isn't as strong as the one that tells him that trusting her is worth the risk.

"Thank you very much, Ma'am" he says, and turns the key.

"Are we going home?" Evie asks.

"Yes," he says.

The woman opens the door to an older gray sedan and waves to them to follow her. She takes a road that leads away from the suburb and then along miles of vineyards and green fields. She turns at last down a deeply rutted lane toward an isolated bungalow in the far distance.

Instead of turning, Nick speeds up and drives straight ahead.

The setting sun burns through Nick's window. The steering wheel is slippery from the sweat on his hands and gritty from the dirt the car has stirred up. He's using all his strength just to stay on the road. Every bone, every muscle, every tendon in his body is commanding him to rest.

The road rises, falls, angles west through the mountains into the blinding setting sun, then swings back north. He drives through small towns, villages, clusters of gas stations and fast food restaurants and mini-malls. While Evie is sleeping, he fills up the gas, gets back into the car, and keeps driving.

There's a figure up ahead at the side of the road. A skinny young boy wearing a sweatshirt and baggy jeans with his thumb out.

Nick pulls over. The boy runs to Evie's window. No, it's a girl, with short strands of hair sticking straight out from under her baseball cap. She looks about fifteen years old.

"Oh my god," Nick says. "Don't you know how dangerous it is for you to be hitchhiking?"

"It's okay. I'm going just past Portland. To see my father," she says.

"We're going up that way. Do you know how to drive?"

"Sure. I drive my uncle's tractor mower all the time."

Nick lets her in and makes sure the mirrors are angled correctly for her. He shows her the gas pedal and the brake and how to put the car in drive. He sits behind her and clutches the back of her seat as she turns the car onto the freeway with a jerk, splaying gravel behind them.

He watches her drive for a few minutes, and when he's confident that she won't steer them off the road, he leans back and closes his eyes. It's wonderful to let someone else take charge for a while, to allow yourself to be carried away, transported. Everything is so easy once you put yourself in someone else's hands. Why had he never realized that before?

It's dark when he wakes up. He listens without opening his eyes.

"You look so familiar," Evie is saying. "Do I know you from the Girls' Home?"

"The Girls' Home?"

"No," Evie says. "Maybe not. I get so confused these days."

"Where are you going?" the girl asks.

"To see my husband. But I don't know where he lives."

"Mm hmmm."

Nick waits for a few minutes before he stretches and opens his eyes. "Where are we?" he asks.

"Almost to the Oregon border."

"I have to go to the bathroom," Evie says.

"We can stop here," the girl offers.

The last time Evie peed by the side of the road was when she was pregnant with Kevin. "I can wait," she says.

They see the warm glow of a diner ahead. "El Rancho" and a rendition of a galloping bull, or possibly a horse, are hand-painted above the door in yellow and red. A low, wide porch stretches across the building. Each of the six windows is a stained glass image of a different kind of beer. Some large black motorcycles lean in a row in front.

The girl pulls over. "This is probably as good as anywhere," she says.

Nick opens his door and almost falls out.

"Whoa, mister." The girl reaches out and steadies him. "You okay?"

"My wife."

"I'll get her."

The girl helps them up the few steps and holds the door open for them.

1983

Less than a year after they were married, Kathy and Mark had a baby girl, Aiden. Nick and Evie drove straight to the hospital in Berkeley that morning.

Kathy was sitting up in bed, nursing her. Mark was examining a disposable diaper. "Nobody told us how to use one of these," he said with some panic in his voice. "I can't even tell which way is which."

"Look," Nick said. "The tape's on the back." He handed it back to Mark and grinned. "Anything else I can help you with, just let me know."

When Aiden was two years old, Mark's computer game venture ended when one of his friends joined the Peace Corps and went to Zambia. Mark joined a software engineering startup. When he began working sixty hours a week, Kathy quit her job to stay home with Aiden and the new baby.

Kevin and Chela graduated from veterinary school, married, and moved to Santa Barbara to open their own clinic. They had a baby boy in 1987.

Nick retired at last and his partner's son took over the law firm. Nick spent his days reading the newspaper and gardening, his new obsession. Evie still took Gracie for a walk almost every morning, but they went more slowly now.

One day, Gracie couldn't stand up. Nick and Evie bundled her up in a blanket and took her to the vet for the last time. Their eyes were dry as they drove home without her.

Evie put her hand on Nick's knee. "So much of life is letting go, isn't it," she said.

He put his hand on hers. "Yes," he said, "but it's easier now."

Still, they could see clearly what was in the other's mind: How could I possibly let go of you?

2000

In May, Kathy and her children, and Kevin and Chela and theirs gathered at Evie and Nick's house for Evie's seventieth birthday party. Nick and Kevin were barbecuing tri-tip, everyone's favorite.

The younger grandchildren were running around the yard with Barney, Aiden's spaniel mix, and Kevin and Chela's big black lab. The older ones were playing video games in the living room.

In the kitchen, Evie, Kathy and Chela were laughing at the stories Evie was telling about Kathy and Kevin when they were children. Suddenly, Evie looked confused.

"Excuse me, dear," she said to Kathy. "I think we've met before, but I don't remember your name."

"What? Mom!" Kathy laughed. "It's me!"

Evie's eyes didn't clear up.

"I think she's serious," Chela murmured to Kathy. "I'm going to get Nick."

"Who are you?" Evie asked again.

Nick, Kevin and Aiden stopped in the doorway.

"I'm Kathy. Your daughter."

"You can't be," Evie said. "I'm sorry, but it's just physically impossible. I would have been about nine years old when you were born."

Evie looked around the kitchen and her eyes lit on Nick. She turned back to Kathy. "You must be Nick's daughter from before we were married," she said. "Oh, my dear, who looked after you for all those years?"

The silence was finally broken by the dogs and the children chasing them through the kitchen.

"Grandma," Aiden said. "Would you like to come and sit outside with me?" She led Evie to one of the patio chairs.

"Something's wrong," Evie said. "What did I say?"

"You forgot Mom's name for a minute," Aiden said. "It's probably because there's so much going on here."

A few weeks later, Evie went out for her morning walk and didn't come back for hours. A neighbor brought her home.

"I was looking for my father," Evie said.

"Your father's been dead for more than twenty-five years," Nick said. "Evie, what's going on?"

"I don't know!"

Nick stroked her hair. "Whatever it is, we can handle it."

Six months after that, just after Thanksgiving, Evie set the stove on fire. She'd decided to surprise Nick and make bacon and eggs for breakfast. She put the package of bacon and three eggs on the kitchen counter. She turned on the front burner and set the fire low. Then she carefully peeled a slice of bacon and placed it on the burner. She peeled a second, and a third and a fourth slice and placed them side by side. She turned around to pick up the eggs, just as a piercing noise overwhelmed the room.

Nick flew into the kitchen from upstairs. "Where's that damned fire extinguisher?" he cried, throwing all the cupboard doors open.

Evie stood paralyzed by the yellow-red flames flickering through the plumes of gray smoke above the stove.

"Turn the smoke alarm off!" Nick shouted. He found the fire extinguisher and sprayed it toward the stove. White foam hissed out and blanketed the stove, the cupboards, the floor.

He climbed up onto the footstool, pulled off the cover of the alarm and yanked out the battery. The last of the smoke faded into wisps that hung from the ceiling like cobwebs. Black streaks fanned up the wall. He collapsed into a chair and looked around the room.

"Evie?"

He found her curled up on their bed.

He sat beside her. "It's okay, Evie. It wasn't your fault."

"It isn't okay," she said. "And it was my fault."

She pulled him down on the bed and pressed her face into his chest.

2001

In January, Evie went to sit down on her chair in the kitchen and it slid out from under her. She fell onto her shoulder and cried out in pain. Brett from down the street took them to the hospital. Nick saw him whisper to the receptionist before he sat down with them.

The emergency room doctor told Nick and Evie that Evie's shoulder was just bruised. After looking at his computer screen for a moment, he sent them to the psychiatrist on call a few doors down the hall.

"I don't need a psychiatrist!" Evie said, outraged. "I've never heard of anything so ridiculous in my life."

The psychiatrist gave her some tests. She failed them all, spectacularly.

"What does that mean?" Nick asked, as they sat facing the doctor across a walnut desk.

"Well," she said, "it looks like Evie has dementia. She might have Alzheimer's disease."

Evie flinched.

"I'll send a copy of my report to your family doctor so he can follow up."

"Whatever the psychiatrist thinks, she's wrong," Nick said on the way home. "We're doing just fine. In fact, I think you're improving."

Once they were home, though, Evie clung to him. "I'm scared, Nick."

"Go upstairs and get into bed," he said. "I'll bring you a cup of tea."

He sat on the edge of their bed while she drank it.

"Will you lie down with me?" she asked.

When she woke up, he was holding her, wanting her.

Chapter Ten

Fall, 2001

The first thing Nick notices about the diner is the smell of beer and cigarette smoke. As his eyes adjust to the dark, he sees that almost everything is dark-stained wood: the tables and chairs, the bar, even the rafters and the underside of the roof. On the floor, straw covers the scuffed planks.

A row of burly men, some of them with ragged beards and long, greasy-looking ponytails, hover over their dark brown bottles at the bar.

"This is my kind of place," Nick tries to joke.

A waitress in a skin-tight, high-cut skirt, a low-cut blouse and ankle boots walks over to them. The men at the bar watch curiously for a moment and then turn back around.

"Hi," she says. "What can I do for you?"

"Do you serve dinner?" Nick asks.

"Just hamburgers and steaks. That okay?"

"That's great."

As they trail behind her, Nick can see through her filmy blouse, a snake's head tattooed just above her skirt. She shows them to a table next to a stained glass window of Moosehead beer.

The hitchhiker pulls Evie's chair out for her and helps her push it back in. The waitress does the same for Nick.

Nick sees Evie pretending to read the menu.

"Would you like a steak and French fries, dear?" he asks her.

"That sounds delicious," she says. "And a glass of red wine."

Nick orders steaks for both of them and the glass of wine, which Dr. Fletcher has forbidden. Nick, feeling reckless, orders a Moosehead for himself. The girl orders a hamburger, fries and a Coke.

Nick leans across the table. Did Kathy ever look that young and vulnerable? He can't remember.

"Well, young lady, since we've put ourselves in your hands, I think we should know your name."

"It's Julie, Sir."

"I'm Nick, and this is—"

"Evie. Yes, Sir." She continues reluctantly. "I saw you on TV."

"We're on TV?" Evie says. "Whatever for?"

Julie leans forward until her fingers almost touch Nick's. "I won't tell. I promise," she whispers.

The waitress brings their meal. The steaks are tender and juicy. The French fries are hand-cut, crunchy on the outside and soft on the inside.

Julie wolfs down her food. She wipes her hand across her mouth, glances at Nick and uses her napkin.

"Would you like another one?" Nick asks.

She eats the second one more slowly and drinks another large Coke.

"Thank you...Nick," she says.

"Do you hear that noise?" Evie interrupts. She's leaning toward the window.

The roar gets louder and stops. The door swings open and one of the men at the bar shouts, "All right! Let's get this party going!"

Ten to fifteen more burly men burst through the doorway and spread out along the bar and at tables across the room.

They're all wearing baggy jeans, white t-shirts and denim jackets with the sleeves cut off. Most have black tattoos around their thick necks and down their muscular arms. A few women come in with them, with big hair and shrunken clothes.

"Hey, boys," the waitress calls, "I thought you weren't coming in tonight."

"If you're here, we're comin'," he laughs.

They joke and talk across the room. One of them turns on the jukebox, loud.

"I wonder what it says on the back of their jackets," Evie says, leaning as closely as she can to Nick's ear.

"Eh?" he shouts back.

"Let's go," she says. "I'm ready to go."

Outside, Nick starts to feel more awake. Stars twinkle. Crickets chirp. He's even starting to enjoy the muffled music and the harsh laughter coming from the bar. He stops on the top step of the porch.

"Look at all those bikes," he says, waving his arm over the two rows of leaning motorcycles. They're Harleys, big ones. And they all have keys hanging from their ignition.

Evie looks at them, and then at him.

Nick looks back at her. "I just want to see how one feels."

He glances at the closed door behind them and casually walks down the steps and over to a bike at the far end of the porch. He picks up a helmet hanging from the handlebar and gives it a disgusted look.

"This looks like a Nazi helmet," he says, and tosses it onto the ground.

"Nick," Julie says in a low voice. "Let's go."

Nick reaches his leg in front of the long leather seat, sits forward and grabs the handlebars. He grins at Evie.

"Come on, get on."

"Nick," Julie says again. "Let's go. Now."

Evie swings her leg over as easily as she did when they were dating, settles onto the seat and wraps her arms around his waist. She rests her head against his back and gives him a little squeeze.

Nick turns the key experimentally and they're almost deafened by the noise. He twists the key back into position. All three of them manage to dive into the bushes in front of the porch before the front door bursts open. Five men lean over the porch.

"Everything looks okay," one of them says at last, and the music fades.

"Are you okay?" Nick whispers.

"Yes," Evie whispers back. "Are you?"

"Yes."

"I'm not," Julie says. "I want to get out of here."

"I have an idea," Nick says. "Come with me."

They creep back to the car. Nick opens the glove compartment and takes out a pen and the vehicle registration card.

"What's your name again?"

"Julie. Why?"

"What's your last name?"

"Owen. Listen, what...?"

Nick waves her away and finishes writing. He holds out the card. "I'm giving you our car," he says. "I don't know how much good this will do you, but you're better off with it than without it."

Julie hesitates. "What are you going to do without a car?"

"You're going to help us steal a motorcycle."

Nick and Julie pull the suitcases out of the trunk of the car and drag them to the motorcycle. They throw as much as they can into the saddlebags and start to push the bike to the side of the road.

"Wait," Evie whispers. "You forgot your helmet."

"I'm not wearing that Nazi helmet," he whispers back.

"You have to." Her whisper becomes more insistent. "It's against the law not to."

"Do you have any idea how many laws I've broken in the last two days?" he whispers fiercely. "They can add it to the list."

Together, Nick and Julie push the motorcycle across the parking lot, past a tall hedge, across another driveway and past a long, low wooden fence. Julie steadies the bike while he and Evie get on.

Nick hands her the car keys and shakes her hand. "My best to you, young lady."

"Thank you, Sir And to you, too."

Nick watches her walk away. When she disappears into the shadows, he turns back to Evie.

"Ready?" he asks.

The noise of the engine shatters the quiet a second time. Moments later, they jerk forward, wobble on the gravel and nearly tip over. Nick finds his balance and they fly down the deserted road. Stars twinkle in the dark sky. Black trees loom over the meadows. The road curves and leads upward into the mountains, leaving the meadows behind. It begins to snake around the cliffs.

Nick follows the white glow of the headlight and leans with the bike into the curves. It knows these roads and it will take them where they want to go. Each bump launches them into the air and propels them forward. The exhilaration is almost painful. They're young lovers again, riding to the beach.

This is her Nick, Evie knows it. She tightens her grip around his waist, presses her head against his back and inhales the smell of him.

She never sees it coming, the hairpin curve. Nick grabs his only chance to save them both. Instead of slowing down and leaning into it, he aims straight for it. The bike clips a pothole, falters and skids off the edge.

As Nick and Evie sprawl through the air, she loses her grip on him. It feels as if she can float forever.

Book Group Questions

Did you enjoy the book? Why or why not? At what point did you decide if you liked it or not? What influenced your decision?

Was there anything unique about the location of the book? Did it enhance or take away from the story?

Can you relate to any of the events in the book? Which ones? Why or why not?

Can you relate to any of the characters? Which ones? Why or why not?

How has Evie's past shaped her life? Nick's?

Do you think their pasts have affected their children?

Do you think what Evie's father said is true: "By my age, everyone is wounded. Some wounds you can see, and some you can't. The ones you can't see are almost always the ones that hurt the most."

What do you think of Evie's choice to cheat on Nick?

If you were Nick, would you have forgiven Evie and gone back to her? Why or why not?

Do you think Nick bears any responsibility for Evie's cheating? Why or why not?

Do you think any actions that you consider immoral or unethical can ever be justified?

How do you feel about the way the story ended?

If you could change something about the book, what would it be? Why?

Is there anyone in this book you would like to meet? What would you ask or say?

If you could be a character in the book, either a new one or one already in the story, what role would you play?

What themes stood out for you? Could you relate to any of them?

Do you have an awareness or an understanding of some aspect of your life that you didn't have before you read this story?

If you were to talk with the author, what would you ask her?

Acknowledgements

Thank you to the members of my writers' group for their generous comments and critiques, and for being so much fun. They are: Petrea Burchard (*Camelot and Vine, Act As If*), Karin Bugge, Linda Dove, Margaret Finnegan (*The Goddess Lounge*), Paula Johnson, Karen Klein and Desiree Zamorano (*Human Cargo, The Amado Women*). Thank you also to my multi-talented daughter, Kim Cheng, and daughter-in-law, Suzie Choi.

I'm very grateful to Howard Simpson of Abba Studios for his skill and patience in designing the cover, logo and interior of the book.

I'd like to thank Kim Cheng and Suzie Choi again, as well as my son Michael and my grandchildren, Emily Cheng, Ian Cheng and Zachary Choi, for filling my life with love.

About the Author

Janet Aird grew up in Montreal, Quebec, mostly, a sophisticated city where she never found her place. What she did discover was writing, especially stories and poetry, and later, songs to play on her six-stringed guitar.

After two years of university in Ottawa, Janet spent a year wandering around Europe, hitchhiking and working from Denmark to Spain to Israel. And writing, writing, writing.

A few weeks after she got back from Europe, she took a Greyhound bus out west and spent a year in Vancouver. She worked as a short order cook in a cafeteria and spent almost all her spare time alone, in the library, walking along the beach, writing in the room she rented in the basement of someone's house.

That summer, Janet took a train back to Montreal. It wasn't long before she headed to the East Coast, to Prince Edward Island, where she met her husband. Two years later, they moved to Halifax, Nova Scotia, where they had two children.

They moved to Los Angeles when the children were in elementary school. The children grew up, and Janet and her husband divorced. She is still writing, now for trade magazines that focus on the environment and sustainability.

Now I Remember I Love You is her first novel.